The Applecross Spell

The Applecross Spell

a novel by

Wendy MacIntyre

Series Editor
Rhonda Bailey

National Library of Canada cataloguing in publication

MacIntyre, Wendy, 1947-

The applecross spell

(Tidelines)

ISBN 1-894852-03-6

I. Title. II. Series : Tidelines (Montréal, Québec).

PS8575.I68A86 2003   C813'.54   C2003-940623-7
PS9575.I68A86 2003
PR9199.3.M32A86 2003

Legal Deposit: Second quarter 2003
National Library of Canada
Bibliothèque nationale du Québec

XYZ Publishing acknowledges the financial support our publishing program receives from the Canada Council for the Arts, the Book Publishing Industry Development Program (BPIDP) of the Department of Canadian Heritage, the ministère de la Culture et des Communications du Québec, and the Société de développement des entreprises culturelles.

Layout: Édiscript enr.
Cover design: Zirval Design
Cover photo: *Morgan-Le-Fay* by Frederick Sandys, Birmingham Museums and Art Gallery

Printed and bound in Canada by Métrolitho
(Sherbrooke, Québec, Canada) in May 2003.

XYZ Publishing   Distributed by: Fitzhenry & Whiteside
1781 Saint Hubert Street   195 Allstate Parkway
Montreal, Quebec H2L 3Z1   Markham, ON L3R 4T8
Tel: (514) 525-2170   Customer Service, tel: (905) 477-9700
Fax: (514) 525-7537   Toll free ordering, tel: 1-800-387-9776
E-mail: info@xyzedit.qc.ca   Fax: 1-800-260-9777
Web site: www.xyzedit.qc.ca   E-mail: bookinfo@fitzhenry.ca

For Heather

Contents

1

The House

Rain sleeked down the tower, like water pouring over the flanks of a horse. The stone was buff pink. In the sunlight, Suzanne remembered, it had had the luminosity, the blush, of healthy flesh.

The tower itself was thirty feet high, topped by a small conical roof shaped like the truncated tip of a dunce's cap. This cap, like the massive roofs of the two main wings of the house, was covered with a dove-grey slate, gone leaden now in the rain.

Yesterday, in a buttery autumn light that had made the pine needles sing silver, Murdo had taken her on a brief tour. His delivery had been perfunctory, yet seamless. Suzanne sensed it had been honed by a hundred repetitions, to visiting colleagues or old school friends. With his mathematician's precision, Murdo had stripped the subject to a few salient points: the age of the house (the tower and east wing dating from the fifteenth century with various additions over the centuries), the number of bedrooms (eight), the minimum thickness of the walls in the original structure (five feet), the size of the grounds (seven acres of mostly tangled woodland, but encompassing also a long-defunct apothecary's garden and a slender tributary of the River Tweed, spanned by a narrow arc of stone barely broad enough to call a bridge).

The house contained "few treasures as such," Murdo said, other than what he described as a "rather baleful Renaissance Madonna," which might or might not belong to the school of Leonardo.

Suzanne's first reaction had been benumbed shock. Murdo had in no way prepared her for the sheer size of the house, nor for its antiquity. "I have a house outside Edinburgh," he had said, a simple enough sentence from which she had conjured up something stolidly bourgeois: three stories of dark hewn stone, the back of a dressing table mirror glowering like a black sun from the top floor bedroom window. This was a furniture arrangement, she had observed on her various stays in the city, much favoured by Edinburgh's middle class. She saw it as a kind of unconscious barricade, the blank face of the mirror pushed tightly against window glass to warn off eyes that might probe the intimacies of bed linen and human nakedness. The city's obsession with propriety had already struck her as strangulation, a kind of small daily death.

Murdo was not Edinburgh-raised. Had he been, Suzanne thought it unlikely that she would have been drawn to him. He had spent his early boyhood in the Caribbean, and so she imagined the boy, so many years before she was born, barefoot on ivory sands, sleeping with cockatoos, dreaming of wild pink blossoms that would forever heat his blood.

He had had, she understood, a most fortuitous deliverance. For his sexuality was cleanly forthright; not the squint-eyed Scots Presbyterian view of the body, all hobbled and grimy with shame.

From their first time together, Murdo had an unfailing capacity to astonish her. Not in the sense of revelations throwing her off balance. Rather, her discovery of some totally new aspect of his experience or character simply reaffirmed for her his apparently fathomless mystery. She realized that she was "in love," and that Murdo's remarkable self-containment had much to do with it. He had an interior vastness, she sensed, that mirrored the sidereal worlds he studied. Ada might have said that he was part of the world of making.

Of course, Suzanne had not had Ada's counsel to bolster her when she made her leap of faith. She had, on the other hand, encountered plenty of external resistance. Several women friends in London had invited her out, or over, for "a drink," shamelessly exploiting her liking for single malts. These encounters had a peculiar sameness. A dispassionate and reasoned prologue, and then the drama itself, in which her friends variously displayed disbelief, anger, and outrage, all mixed with plentiful libations. They had all in the end wished her well, while making their reluctance quite evident. Their tighter-than-usual ritual hugs saddened her. She saw that they wanted her to recant (Charlotte Meredith, who belonged to a feminist theatre troupe, had done a charming pantomime of begging on her knees, which had made them both laugh) and that they saw her decision as heresy. And then there was Gemma's reaction. But Suzanne still could not bear to think too much of Gemma.

Although she did not encourage them, she knew her friends saw her as a sort of figurehead. Her books had been well reviewed, and more importantly, they were popular, partly because of her lavish use of illustrations. She had herself always loved picture books. She was a feminist "name," although certainly not a star. Not that she would have wished such a status. She did what she did, delighting – almost too much so – in the research, poring over physical images of women produced over the centuries. These were images, wrought mainly by men, that women throughout the Western world had absorbed – often, as Suzanne tried to show, to their own cost. Her first book was titled *The Whore*, its longest chapter devoted to Mary Magdalene. Her second, *The Maiden*, had gone into three reprints.

She had not been surprised to find neither of her works for sale in Edinburgh's most comprehensive book store. Not that it much mattered. She had her research for her next book to begin, and her life with Murdo. She did believe that she had purged herself of all doubts. Sometimes she recalled with hurt anger the most extreme of the reactions to her decision. On three separate occasions, radical feminists of her acquaintance had cut her dead on the street. To marry, she understood, was to move beyond the pale.

She savoured the irony. For this was what she desired. A migration beyond her known world that would match her leap of faith. Never – before Murdo – had she conceived of marriage with a man as a possibility in her own life. Certainly, the words "husband" and "wife" were anathema to her: the one with its insidious implications of management and control; the other so stripped of character and particularity that a woman was speedily objectified. She hated most the way some men would refer to "the wife," as if they said "the table" or "the fire grate."

Murdo had understood when she explained that these were loaded terms, that would burrow like worms into the life of their relationship. "But of course," he had said. "Of course." He had regarded her so gravely, she had been momentarily mesmerized by the golden flecks in his eyes. A second later it occurred to her that she might perhaps have been insensitive. He was after all twice widowed. "Wife" might therefore be a holy word to him. Doubly so, and fraught with pain. But he had smiled, and taken her hand, so that she knew by his silence all was well.

It was a "marriage" she wanted, a word that was for her numinous and honeycombed with light. She was aware that she had probably sucked in these mystical associations with her mother's milk. She had grown up surrounded by Ada's tomes of magic and theosophy. Isis and Osiris were as real to her as the man who delivered the bread or the foreign sailors she and Ada saw when they walked down to the Halifax harbour.

Suzanne had believed in that divine couple, as much as she had in the conjoining of Solomon and Sheba. This was the union of irreconcilables Ada spoke of: "Opposites underpin the world, Suzanne." This saying was indelibly linked with an engraving, whose tissue-thin protective covering Ada would lift carefully with the tip of her fingernail. Here was the female Water, her hair a torrent that streamed down her back, and then curved upward to embrace the male body of Fire. Water streamed too from her fingertips, as flame did from his. They were depicted in profile, their faces tranquil and human, their eyes locked in love.

The first time Suzanne saw Murdo, she had seen in him that old childhood image of the male Fire. Murdo's abundant hair massed in waves that called to mind a slow-burning bed of flame. Only in stark daylight did one notice the streaks of grey amidst the red-gold. Her first time in bed with him, it had seemed only right that he had radiated such heat against the coolness of her flesh.

None of these things could she confide to any of her women friends, most especially the mystical groundwork she had inherited from Ada.

"Everything that is holy, is secret." Another of Ada's precepts. So Suzanne had kept secret, even from Murdo, the most compelling of her reasons for marrying. She could never have said aloud: I love you for your mystery and your silence and the fact that your spirit has been tempered by much suffering. To speak that would have trammelled it. The utterance itself might well kill love.

Watching the rain sleek down Murdo's tower, she could, for a moment, believe herself in a dream. Here she was, standing in front of a Gothic structure in a man's vermilion rain slick that reeked of pipe tobacco. Even the umbrella she held was a sort of surreal creation, its ivory handle yellowing like old teeth, its mammoth dome alternating segments of orange and lime-green. Worse, she had discovered the umbrella in a hall stand that had obviously once been an elephant's foot. The thought of it made her shudder. Had Ada been there, Suzanne was sure she would have performed a purifying ritual over this cruelly offensive object, exorcising the beast's final pain that clung still in the hair.

Tomorrow she would tell Murdo that she would like the thing moved out of sight.

Suddenly, as though prompted by a dream-like illogic, she experienced an irresistible urge to lay her cheek on the wet stone of the tower. She drew back at once, because where she had anticipated smoothness, there was a rasp of stucco against her skin.

2

A New Bride

Murdo mistrusted words. Once he had confided to her that he considered language a kind of neurotic babbling, a peculiarly human disease. Sound, syllable, sense, all paled beside the flawless arabesques of his equations. These symbols, whose meaning was forever locked away from her, sometimes resembled stark-branched trees, or the spiny ferns that frost scribes on a window. They had the sharp-edged delicacy of winged insects. Suzanne could imagine them wafted in by a south-borne wind, settling themselves on the page in groupings that matched the design in Murdo's brain. Were she to pick up the piece of paper and shake it, they might well fly off, and write their secret elsewhere.

When she pictured his formulae in this way, she could more easily understand how words might seem to him clumsy, heavy things that encumbered the tongue. Indeed, in the weeks after they were married, he spoke to her less than when they had first met. Suzanne accepted this as part of the structure of their being together, a companionable silence that flowered daily in ways she had not anticipated. She took a real sensual pleasure, for example, in the gestural play of his fingers, a manual dance that mirrored the tentative testing, then the buoyant surge, of his mental calculations. He would become so totally absorbed, his long fingers weaving invisible architectonics in the air, that she felt she witnessed an intensely private ritual.

There was a storybook element in their silent companionship as well. For so much did Murdo's broad, sculpted face resemble a lion's, she sometimes imagined she had tumbled with him into a world where beasts walked and talked and dreamt of Platonic forms.

His body too, had a leonine muscular tautness, and there was an underlying tawny hue to his skin. In bed he continued to radiate that almost fierce desert heat she found both sensual and comforting, for in Britain it seemed she was never quite warm enough, despite duvets and the hot water bottle she tucked under her feet. At night sometimes, he would wake her with a restless tossing, or an arm flung out suddenly. When she touched him then he would be feverish, and she understood that in dreams, he was reliving some old suffering. The loss of his first wife. Or the second. Or most painfully, dreams of the two together. It pleased her then to comfort him, to wrap her arms about him as though he were a child she was easing out of the grip of a nightmare. The fact he was twenty-eight years her senior would strike her most sharply then. It meant he had had so much more time to accumulate pain, in which fate had cruelly conspired.

She did not pity him. To pity, she realized, would poison love. Nor did she pry. She had had relationships, even with women, where the dedication to "honesty," the too deliberate stripping away of each other's facades and defences, had resulted in a mutual contempt. One must accept the vast inner darkness of one's lover, she told herself. He would tell her what he chose in his own good time. These were the guidelines she set herself.

Meanwhile, she relished their easy silences. When Murdo did speak, she sensed he selected his words with tact and sensitivity paramount. Unlike the sureness of their physical lovemaking, his speech with her was often tentative. It was as though he saw the invisible relation between them as a new and tender organism that even his breath might harm.

So that she was profoundly taken aback when on the third morning at his Scottish Borders house, he asked her a question she considered both blunt and intrusive. They were sitting in the garden behind the house. The day was almost hot, the sky an unmarked azure. The weather seemed to Suzanne miraculously un-Scottish. Earlier, from the window of her study, she had seen the triple crown of the Eildon Hills free of cloud shadow. The clear light clung to their green like silk.

Murdo had on a broad-brimmed Panama hat so that his face was shaded from her when he asked abruptly: "Can you have children?"

She did not know then why she did it. Perhaps it was the rage she felt flaming in her head. It was not so much the question itself that set her anger off, as his tone. Challenging? Sly? Whichever, she disliked it intensely. The garden changed suddenly. Murdo might have been a sadistic jailer subjecting her to interrogation. The sun was spoiled for her. It was a bare bulb now, in a caged lamp he thrust near her eyes. So she lied. "No," she said, certain that he would believe her. She had learned long ago that it was essential in life to know how to lie well.

"So," he said. It was a word Murdo much favoured. Like Q.E.D., it seemed to signify closure for him, the proof accomplished. So.

"Is it a problem?" she asked, making no effort to hide her irritation.

"Of course not," he replied. "No, of course not."

He crossed over to her chair, drew her up by the hand. She pushed back the niggardly thought that this was a learned, courtly gesture. As he held her, and her own body registered his familiar heat, she felt her annoyance melt away.

She had misinterpreted, she thought, been overly sensitive. It was sometimes an unfortunate adjunct of feminism, this excessive defensiveness. Like those women friends who suggested she perceived in Murdo the father she had never had. Warning of dangers. Of the inevitable erosion of her own power. Suzanne believed they were wrong. On the other hand, she was aware, as was every thinking woman, that she must stay vigilant.

Later that day as she worked through the reproductions she had collected so far, renderings of seductive witches, hideous hags, Macbeth's three sisters huddled over their cauldron, she found herself remembering with satisfaction her first act she had consciously kept secret from Murdo. She had had an intense need simply to do something covert, a deed without his knowledge.

It happened in Amsterdam, where they went for three days immediately following their marriage in a North London registry office. She did not think of it as a honeymoon, a word she found sickly and loathsome. Simply, it was their first trip away together, a kind of symbolic removal from the British Isles.

They followed the concentric windings of the canals, where one morning they saw a new bride being photographed, her veil flowing out behind her over the water. By unspoken agreement, they avoided the Red Light district. Suzanne had never had any desire to see it. Intuitively she knew that Murdo would have found any proximity to such voyeurism degrading.

On their second afternoon in Amsterdam, Murdo fell asleep in their hotel room. The book he had been reading dropped from his hand to the floor. Suzanne felt the impulse seize her then, and slipped out.

She knew where to go. Her destination was only a few blocks from their hotel. The sweetly acrid scent hit her as soon as she opened the café door. The place was tiny. There were five tables surrounded by high stools, and a coffee bar tucked into the back corner, with a list of the extremely limited fare posted on the wall behind. Suzanne nodded to the woman behind the counter, and walked directly to the spiral staircase that led to the café's upper reaches. There she found a handsome black man with a menu.

She perused it and asked for a gram of Afghani black. Downstairs she purchased papers and a coffee from the bar, and sat down to roll herself a joint. As she smoked it, she wondered whether Murdo would disapprove. She felt high, jubilant, in part because she had needed this separateness from him. The joint was a kind of ritual self-celebration. She did not consider it at all childish.

Walking back to the hotel, she was struck by the outer gleam of the barges and their inner secrecy. Gulls swooped like manic angels. The ebb and flow of the water matched the rhythm of her blood. Then she saw the bride again. Or rather, she caught a glimpse of the billowing white veil just behind her right shoulder. Yet when she turned around, there was nothing, no one there. As she walked on, it appeared again, a kind of massed shimmering whiteness at the edge of her vision. She attributed the illusion to the potency of the hashish, took a few deep breaths and went on. This time the veil disappeared.

Until, later that night at dinner, it showed up again, hovering over Murdo's shoulder just as he raised his wine glass to his lips. She remained quite calm, telling herself it was just the residual effects of the drug.

There was, however, another possibility. If it were so, she had married far more than she had bargained for. At that moment, she wished desperately that her mother were still alive.

3

Her Mother's Teachings

It was Ada who had inspired Suzanne's book on the "Whore," a fact in which she considered herself fortunate. How many women had mothers who could help them redeem *whore* from the muck heap, stripping it of overlays false and foul, until it was set in their midst again, shining?

Not that this redemption had been a painless process. Once, Suzanne might have said that the cost was too high, too personal; even bloodied. For there had been a time – her tenth year in particular – when physical battle had been a daily event. All that September and October, she came home from school to pluck gravel from her knees, elbows, or palms. Ada bathed the wounds, patted on the yellow-green unguent of her own making; then wrote invisibly on her daughter's brow the arcane symbols that would help her endure the next day's torment.

"They are ignorant and to be pitied," Ada said of Suzanne's assailants. These trials would make her strong, Ada insisted. Tears were pointless. "Think of the magic cauldron," Ada said, tilting Suzanne's chin upward with a long white finger, tipped with a carmine nail. "You have to plunge into the boiling water and take the pain, to be made new and courageous."

"You'll have a life-power they will some day envy," Ada insisted. "Poor little insects," she added, with a click of her tongue. For Ada, all lesser mortals – namely, those she judged to be motivated primarily by cruelty, greed, or wilful stupidity – were insects.

"Not to hate. Not to hate. That's the thing. And avoid striking back if you can. There are other ways. You will find other ways." Her milk-white hands would cup Suzanne's chin. Her mother's hands about her face were veined petals, and she – Suzanne – was a flower closing for the night. There was honey in her blood.

At ten she knew, as she knew ever after, how blessed she was to have a mother who could work spells.

"I want to kill them," she told Ada once, wincing not so much at the washing out of the wound, as at the remembered words. "Your mother's a whore." Only it came out "whirr" in their small, red mouths. "She sells her bum. She sells her bum." They would push out their little rear-ends at her, as well as their tongues; then rush her with bodies hard as bulls, four or five of them in a phalanx. Always girls. The boys were largely indifferent, contributing only the odd snigger.

Her habitual attackers were a group of five girls, all relishing a complex thrill that mixed moral superiority, sadism, and the mysterious electricity of sex. How had they imagined it, Suzanne wondered years later. A monstrous male god perhaps, with lascivious slanting eyes and horny unstoppable hands that groped for their virgin bodies in the dark. His name was Sex. His blood was hot. He had all whores in his thrall.

As a child, she had understood that in calling Ada a whore they were simply repeating what they had heard their parents say. Or to be charitable, perhaps only one parent of one girl, and so it had spread as malicious words will, flicking from tongue to tongue.

"Whirr. Whirr. Wriggles her bum. Wriggles her bum." Their little bodies writhed. They looked like pale snakes in the sun. Then they became bulls again, rushing her. Suzanne tasted blood in her mouth.

"I want to kill them," she said. It was for Ada's sake she wished them ill. She wanted vengeance for Ada, whose long, strong-boned face was sometimes a Gypsy's, sometimes a Russian ballerina's. Ada with her straight spine and purposeful stride. Who wore clothes that flowed about her as she moved. Who had never wriggled her bum in her life.

"Revenge is its own poison," Ada cautioned. "You can be angry at the pitiful little insects. But *use* the anger. Use its power to help you walk straight and stay proud. Keep him bridled, for Anger's a potent and slippery demon. He'll swell like a puffed-up toad if you don't keep the bridle on. Then he'll get control of you."

Living with Ada, Suzanne inhabited a world populated with demons (or daimons as her mother often called them), powers that could be summoned for good or ill. Everything had its own daimon: spices and trees and balls of opaque glass; shells and bells and swatches of velvet or linen. Emotions. Water. Fire.

Ada belonged to no school, neither Gardnerian nor Alexandrian witchcraft. She was a syncretist, as eclectic as Madame Blavatsky, but without the chicanery. At heart, she was an animist. When Ada looked at a stone, she saw a being that lived and breathed. Stones sometimes spoke, she told Suzanne. That was why, if you arranged them in just such a way, in configurations the stones themselves suggested, they would yield you such power. Sometimes Ada added incense and music, Dufay and Palestrina, to bring about a wedding of sensations, a synaesthesia so total that when it peaked, the world was drenched in colour. Suzanne remembered once riding the chrome-yellow surge of sound issuing from a crumhorn. It bore her up through the window. She had the buoyancy, the energy, of a darting sunbeam. Afterward, her sleep was profound.

Yet there were times when Suzanne found Ada's presence overwhelming. Even when sitting perfectly still, her long eyes closed, Ada could project an urgent agitation, a kind of raw energy that reddened the air about her. Did she battle demons at these times, or plumb the depths of another soul to seek the source of its pain, as one would draw a thorn from flesh? Suzanne was never to know. She was aware only that she must absent herself when Ada was in these states. For to stay could be terrifying, in a room so charged that it would begin to throb.

Ada had many faces, and was in fact a consummate actress. She could play the haughty Queen of Pentacles (there were clients who came simply because they thrilled to this performance); or Compassionate Confidante and Gentle Healer.

Then there was the sleek Gypsy Sorceress, from whose hands the cards flowed like settling doves. For this role, Ada gathered her dark hair into a taut braid that brushed the small of her back. She had an array of embroidered silk shawls, all with the deep black fringe that elongated her already sinuous movements. Her hooped earrings were huge; some plain gold, some engraved with scarabs or twined snakes, some studded with diamantes that caught the light from the candles she would set about her consulting room. The curtains in this room were always drawn, so that with candles or sometimes oil lamps, she could reproduce the half-light of dusk or dawn. These were the times of potency, Ada explained, when the spirits moved most easily between our world and their own.

None of these trappings were specious. Not the beaded curtain that hung in the doorway to the reception room, and which Ada would open with a flourish, gesturing the client through. Certainly not the whisk broom ("My besom," Ada called it) that was always propped in one corner of the living room. This broom was never used for sweeping. Suzanne understood very early that the besom was in some sense a revered object, much as the crucifix and family Bible were in more conventional Halifax homes. Later, she understood it purely as a symbol of a sisterhood that stretched back centuries.

Ada was respectfully cautious with her own gifts, and to have engaged in any sort of charlatanism would likely have killed her. She had, for example, no crystal ball. "Swami stuff," she called such practices. Any duping of the public, she found repugnant.

Ada could – and did – give readings of personal destinies using either the Egyptian Tarot or a standard deck of cards. She rejected the reading of palms as pure theatrics. Sometimes, she would agree to help clients explore past lives. She also had an unfailing ability to locate lost objects, and on many occasions, missing persons. This visualization process involved a concentration so intense that she appeared to be in pain, eyes screwed shut, knuckles pressed into her temples.

One of her greatest gifts was comforting the bereaved, a talent that made her even more unpopular with the local clergy. Ada took care to undercut no one's gods, unless she honestly believed their effects were pernicious. Her syncretism admitted them all, and she would not hesitate to bring in elements of her clients' faiths if she felt this would help them cope. In extreme cases, she would act as a conduit between the bereaved and the spirit of the deceased. This was not a task she took on lightly. For one thing, she found such communication physically and psychically draining. She believed, as well, that one should avoid disturbing the newly dead, if at all possible. If they came first to you, that was another matter.

For clients' physical ailments, Ada maintained a pharmacopoeia of tisanes, ointments, and rubbing oils. Some of these compounds were based on the lore of her beloved Marsilio Ficino; others were drawn from the tradition of Wicca (the

Craft, Ada called it); some were her own invention. She had efficacious cures for impetigo, eczema, arthritis, and pinkeye. The client's belief was a necessary component in all her cures, most especially when she worked with phobias. Ada was an instinctual therapist, with an unstinting compassion and an adamantine power of the will.

Her clientele came from all segments of Halifax society: working-class women out of their own neighbourhood, society matrons who always wore dark glasses, real estate salesmen and stockbrokers seeking the foreknowledge that would make them rich (what Ada really gave them was self-confidence). Then there were the foreign sailors, very often Russians and Poles, who would return each year. They were attracted to her exoticism, for Ada was a rarity in Halifax; and she in turn was drawn to their rugged darkness, their wide, high cheekbones that seemed to pierce the air, and their ingrained restlessness. Through them Ada was able to satisfy her own wanderlust vicariously. Intuitively, Suzanne realized how the world sometimes tugged at her mother. She could readily picture Ada in the classic, circus-bright horse-drawn caravan, following the twists of roads that wound ahead of her like smoke. The sailors of whom Ada was fondest had been to Peking, to Kashmir, to the Caucasus where Zeus, she told Suzanne, had chained Prometheus to a rock for daring to steal fire from the gods. The sailors brought bottles of glittering vodka that itself tasted like fire.

Sometimes one of the sailors would spend the night. It was these liaisons, together with visits from other males among Ada's varied clientele, that fuelled the gossip she was a whore.

Whores, Ada carefully explained to Suzanne, had once been holy women, celebrated in their own temples, superbly knowledgeable about the transports and dangers implicit in the act of sex. It was male greed that had undermined the sacredness of these temple whores, Ada said. Male greed and the terrible imbalance of power between men and women in this world.

Such were the roots of Suzanne's feminism, with the archetypes of witch and whore made living presences through the heat of her mother's belief. When she read the myth of Athena springing full-grown from the forehead of Zeus, Suzanne automatically transposed the story to herself and to Ada. Ada's strength and her flaunting of convention made this kind of parthenogenesis seem quite likely. Nor could Suzanne ever remember feeling genuinely deprived because she had no father.

"He was a sailor," Ada told her, "and he died." She would say no more, and there were no telling photographs or keepsakes. One did not push with Ada.

If Suzanne sometimes found her upbringing bizarre, if she sometimes said things to Ada that years later made her writhe in shame, ultimately she saw their relationship as beyond price. For Ada did not seek deliberately to mould and shape her, as Suzanne observed happening with so many of her friends. Other parents prodded and poked, and threatened their children with the withdrawal of affection.

Ada believed the nuclear family was responsible for much psychic damage. She was an R. D. Laing enthusiast, finding in his books a poetic expression of her own sense of things: that what masqueraded as familial love was often a form of violence.

Ada had chosen Suzanne's name to reflect her deep mistrust of the conventional family. Her daughter's namesake was a young medieval Scotswoman, Suzanne Clelland, immortalized in a Border Ballad. That Suzanne had fallen in love with one of the enemy – an Englishman. Despite her parents' pleading, she would not give up her lover. It was her own mother and father who dragged her to the stake to be burned for her treachery. The Suzanne Clelland of the old

Ballad did not recant. She freely chose the flame rather than forsake her chance at love.

"The name is your amulet," Ada instructed her. "Keep it. Never change it."

This caution was as much information as Ada would ever venture about Suzanne's future. Although she was sometimes willing to predict the fates of her clients, she would not do so for her own daughter. Maternal love would interfere with her clairvoyance, she said.

"Your name is your amulet. Never change it," was all Ada would say.

So that on her marriage to Murdo Napier in a North London registry office, she did not even consider any of the unwieldy compounds that might have assuaged her feminist principles: not Clelland-Napier or Napier-Clelland. Instead she signed – as she was to sign all her life – the name Suzanne Clelland.

4

The Signs

Murdo drew his latest equation on her body with the tip of his index finger. She shivered, closed her eyes, tried to picture the invisible signs he traced over and over, on the skin of her breasts, her belly, her inner thighs.

Suzanne sped back to childhood. It was Ada's feathery touch she felt, forming the protective symbols on her forehead, and at her temples and wrists where the pulse of blood would help absorb the charm. Anodyne. She had learned the word first from Ada. It had its own magic coolness and controlled power, like a crystal drop suspended in a blue glass vial. Or sometimes she pictured a solitary pearl on the beach, made hard and shining by the sea. The bed sheets smelled of the sea, for Ada hung them out to dry in the brisk wind that came from the harbour.

Comforted, protected, and strong. Her eyes closed, the better to savour and memorize the sweet drift of her mother's touch. Tucked in clean sheets, she would feel the day's grubbiness, all the small failures and humiliations, drain away. The bedtime magic was her most intensely private ritual with Ada. She would experience then the sheer intensity of her mother's powers. She was never able to describe exactly what it was happened. Yes, it was a current flowing into her, but more like water than electricity, coursing and then lapping through her veins. Yet there was also fire, the vivid sparks Ada implanted in her mind that Suzanne sensed were the sureness of all her possibilities to come. There was air too, for just before sleep, she would feel herself floating, skimming the surface of clouds. And at the close of this ritual, Ada brought in the certain solidity of earth. Curled on earth's breast, Suzanne need never fear falling, that sickening plummet that sometimes came in dreams.

Earth, Water, Fire, and Air. Suzanne knew these were the Elements of the Wise. If she wanted to draw on their powers, she had to picture them clearly first. Vis-u-al-ize, Suzanne. Ada sounded it out for her. Visualization was one of the most important parts of magic. If Suzanne wanted something to happen, she had to make the picture of it in her mind's eye, as perfectly exact as possible, the colours throbbing, with all the pointed detail she could muster.

Ada had stopped this ritual just about the time Suzanne started to menstruate. The blood meant she was growing up. Now she must protect herself, transform the day's trials into strength as best she could. The Elements were also called the Four Watchtowers, and so Suzanne visualized herself as a strong, squared keep, a fastness on which each year she would build higher. She pictured it ultimately, set as high as Citadel Hill. Sometimes she surveyed the city from her imagined prospect, her eyes taking in only those places she loved best: her mother's clapboard house, the Old Burying Ground at the corner of Barrington Street, and the mouth of the harbour itself, where the waves crashed forever against the rocks.

Her imagined keep had ramparts she paced, not restlessly, but with pride, visiting each of the Watchtowers in turn. She had entered a stage in life where she must be wary, with her body changing, becoming soft and desirable. There was a big difference, Ada said, between caution and a hampering fear.

Certainly not all men were bad. But it was best to be on one's guard.

Suzanne cultivated the image of the squared, strong keep. And in a kind of consonant magic, her legs grew longer, her body supple and resilient. She learned early that she could outpace men who pestered her on the street. She did not have to run. A brisk walk was enough. Usually, they faltered, lagged, pouted, and faded away. When needed, she could assume a hauteur that made the most ardent pest wither in his tracks. Once, she tried out high heels; then abandoned them forever. They slowed her; and would most certainly impede flight. She avoided compromising situations. And prayed luck would be on her side. Because there were many ways, including brute force, that one might find oneself undone. "Be wary but unafraid," Ada said. "The signs will stay with you always." The invisible, protective symbols were a gift for life. From mother to daughter. Long fingers tracing the whorls of the electromagnetic currents of Earth, the loopings up to the stars and back.

"So elegant and so sexy," Murdo said. She came speeding back through time, her body shuddering luxuriously with the warmth of his breath in the hollow of her ear. This bed. Murdo's fingers.

The overlapping of her childhood with the present had been so seamless. Like travelling the inner and outer curves of a Möbius strip. Murdo had made one just the other day, snipping a band of unvarying width from the top of *The Scotsman*, and twisting it, just so, into that one-sided model of infinity. His brow furrowed as he studied it, as though the thing itself perplexed him. Then he flicked the strip into the fire (the morning was thickly damp), where it crisped and crumbled into a fine black ash.

"We are all such," he said, head lowered to watch the ash disperse through a red gorge of flame. The lines in his brow deepened. As if he were a man of clay, Suzanne thought, and the thought itself were a sharp instrument that scored the gouge between his eyes. Paradoxically, she knew she would never have married him but for that so-evident pain; for his tragedies that separated him out from the mass of men. The vagaries of life had made tender hollows in him, visible and invisible.

She went and stood behind his chair, her breasts pressed against his shoulders. The ease of their bodies together, the many perfect ways they fit, still amazed her. This fittingness itself seemed a kind of gnosis, a secret knowledge that contained worlds.

"So elegant and so sexy," Murdo repeated. Did he mean her or his equation? He would often define a formula as "sexy." This was his ultimate approbation. Suzanne would sometimes try to imagine what it was he saw in his mind's eye, but could get no further than a curve or loop of radiant light. It would be spare, certainly. Quintessential form, all unnecessary detail pared away.

She supposed that her own slimness pleased Murdo for just that reason. That her "elegant lines" as he described them, matched his mathematical ideal. This appreciation she interpreted as yet another facet of the rightness of their union, as if he had already imagined her, held the shape of her in his mind, long before they actually met. So that coming to him was, in a sense, coming home.

Unfortunately, there was a cruel aspect to Murdo's admiration for structural spareness. She had witnessed it on several occasions, once in a café in Amsterdam, when a portly young man with a protuberant belly sat at an adjacent table and Murdo had made a pointed remark. More recently, she and Murdo had passed a trio of tourists in the High Street, three women, all quite overweight, and puffing audibly from the exertion of their climb up to the Castle. Suzanne noted with distaste the nasty curl of Murdo's lip, a sneer superior as a schoolboy's, as he watched their laboured progress. On both occasions, she had remonstrated with him later, for she found such condescension childish and reprehensible. And both times, he had affected not to know what she was talking about. In fact, he became quite irritated, so much so that she let the matter drop. This was a small enough flaw, she reasoned, a mere peccadillo and nothing she should let spoil what was essentially an expansive bliss.

This happiness carried over into their respective work, where she sensed a subtle and continuous cross-fertilization. When Murdo spoke to her of the search for a unified field theory, or of Gödel's Theorem, or of the fact that subatomic particles can travel backward in time/space, the wonder in his eyes was telling. Suzanne understood that she and Murdo were each set on the same daunting task: to see their subject whole. In his case, this was the physical cosmos. In hers, the human psyche.

Certain of her colleagues became irritated whenever Suzanne spoke of her "larger" vision. A feminist's sole and proper study should be women, they said. Women's souls and bodies and circumstances. Not men's souls. If indeed, men had souls. And they would sniff at the air derisively in that conditioned response Suzanne had come to find so very tiresome. Of course, she saw their point. Much that men had done – and still did – disgusted and appalled her. Yet she chose to believe in the possibility of a redemptive transformation, if not for every man; then at least, for particular individuals. She chose to believe too, that there did exist the rare exceptions – like Murdo – men who did not seek to diminish women, who knew just how intricate was the balance of their respective powers.

This was a holy business, a fact that Murdo tacitly recognized. There was no other way it could be described.

She rejoiced too, in Murdo's evident sympathy and compassion. For she was finding much of her research even more gruelling than she had anticipated. She had to force herself to a full imagining of her subjects' pain; she owed them nothing less. She learned with some discomfort that torture to extract "confessions" from witches had been far more commonplace in Scotland than in England. The instruments the Scottish inquisitors used had their own horrific symbolism; the form embodying the ultimate aim – that all women be silent and biddable. If not, they must be broken. And so there was the "witch's bridle," an iron collar and gag that clamped about a woman's face; and the metal shoe and brace, that when tightened, could crush and maim a woman's foot. And of course, the long, piercing bodkin of the witch-pricker, who thrust his needle into the most tender parts of a woman's body, seeking out the devil's marks.

Women had undergone these agonies of flesh and spirit mere miles from where she now sat, reading and turning away from the reading, digging her fingernails into her palms in some paltry and totally meaningless act of sympathy.

In her dreams, the smell of burnt flesh was sometimes overwhelming. Murdo was kind when she cried out in her sleep and woke him. He put his brow to hers as if to cancel out these terrible images through the simple touch of love. His arms about her made a loose wreath. Instinctually, he understood that she could not have borne any tightness, the strictures that might evoke the clamps and bodkins and the final binding to a hewn stake above a laid pyre.

Hundreds of women had been burned on Edinburgh's High Street. Each time Suzanne passed the brooding grey bulk of St. Giles Cathedral, she would think of the evil box it once had housed. A box with a slit, nasty as pursed lips, to receive accusations against women believed to be witches. Fashioned no doubt by the same industrious carpenter who made the fornicator's stool, set up near the front of the kirk, where the wicked might be in full view.

She thanked heaven Murdo had escaped that inheritance. And that he was what he was.

Suzanne took to wandering the grounds behind the house. She grew restless when she worked, her long legs cramping if she sat too long. Walking helped her order her thoughts, comb through the profuse contradictions her research uncovered about the witch archetype.

The witch was either nubile, naked, with high pointed breasts and silken limbs, and an enticing smile that promised fleshly delights; or she was the typical crone, hunched, long nose hooking over scraggly lips, toothless or single-toothed, wizened and dun-coloured, like a twisted root that has lain long underground. Often terrifying, with glint-hard eyes. No succour here. She swoops into children's dreams, shattering their pure sleep with her cackle. She beckons the tender Hansel and Gretel with her bony finger, luring them to their doom. Even when she is comic, she is still horrific. Like the hag who pursued the cloyingly virtuous Little Lulu. Tsk. Tsk. Always returning, no matter how often she was foiled. As she does each North American Halloween, her craggy silhouette incised against an orange backdrop. Or in a rubber mask, the face warty and deformed, topped by a fright wig.

Yet the power of the archetype endured. As the words associated with her endured. Hag. Join this with "fag," and you got in two shots at once. And the word witch itself rhymed so very readily with bitch.

On the apparently plus side, there were "enchanting" and "bewitching" and the ubiquitous "glamour," which had once meant the casting of a spell. Yet Suzanne sensed an underlying mistrust in all these supposedly positive attributes. As if this compelling sensuality had been got through an underhand

trick. Legerdemain. Or a pact with dark forces. Glamour
means that all is not as it appears. The silken thighs may well
conceal a vagina dentata.

The siren enchantress and the withered crone were in
fact the same person. This had been brought home to her
very clearly indeed by a Goya engraving. An old witch is
instructing a young witch. They are both naked, the crone
the pilot, the apprentice nestled behind her, on a broomstick
soaring up through a louring sky. The contrast between the
two women's bodies is shocking. The neophyte has the
unmarked flesh, the generous hips and breasts, the wasp
waist, of an Arabian houri. Her instructor seems to be shaped
of melting wax, all drooping dugs and flaccid buttocks. The
nose is a cruel hook. There is not an inch of her that is
unwrinkled. But the two bodies are contingent, their postures identical, so that one sees clearly that the elder is the
shadow of the younger. The crone is what the delectable
houri will become.

And many of us still fear it, thought Suzanne. We fear
turning into the hag.

Suzanne was stopped abruptly in her thoughts by the sight
of an ancient outbuilding just to the right of her path. On first
glance, the roof of this structure appeared to have an abundance of thick hair. On closer inspection, she saw this "hair"
was actually a thriving spiny bush that had rooted itself under
the dirt between the slates. Unlike Murdo's house, the stone
of the outbuilding was not a homogenous buff, but dappled,
brown and beige, so that its front resembled the open, freck-
led face of a child. There was a single circular window, like a
third eye, set right in the centre of the second storey, under the
roof. The building had two wooden doors, set about five feet
apart, each surrounded by a recessed stone arch.

Curious to see inside, she chose the door on the right,
set beneath the most profuse of the hair-like growth on the
roof. She lifted the latch and then gave the door a push,

jumping well clear in case there were any loose stones in the lintel. The heavy door swung inward surprisingly easily, revealing a soft inner gloom. She was reminded of the mysteriously dusky backgrounds of Rembrandt so that she half expected to see an Esther or a placid Jewish bride materialize in the foreground.

Listening carefully, she waited a moment before crossing the threshold. The place had the look of being long abandoned. A fox or a badger might have made its home here. She clapped her hands sharply three times, then listened again for any telltale rustle or snarl. Reassured by the continuing silence, she moved forward, peering into the shadowy interior. At first, she could make out no shape at all. There was only the smell, a meld of dank earth, mouldering hay, and the scent of lamp oil. As her eyes gradually adjusted, she saw an oil lamp hanging from the hook beside the door. She took the lamp down and carried it outside. The wick looked healthy, and there was enough oil left to yield a decent light. Luckily, she had a small box of Bluebell matches in her jacket pocket, together with a packet of five cigarettes, still in their cellophane wrapping. Although she had long ago given up smoking, she liked to keep these with her as a comfort, and a visible reminder of what discipline could accomplish.

She lit the lamp and carried it inside, watching the golden light seep outward and up the stone walls. What she saw first was a sturdy ladder leading up to a loft, heaped with old straw.

Looking down, she saw that the earthen floor had been tamped so that it had the consistency of hard clay. Whose feet had tramped it, she wondered, and how long ago? At first she thought the room was quite bare, until, turning toward her left, she saw an old plank table set tight into the corner. On top of the table was a bulky object, swathed in sheets of dull plastic.

Setting the lamp on the table, she began to unwind the plastic sheeting to see what it concealed. At no point then did it occur to her that she was being intrusive. Had she found the package in Murdo's study, or in the tower-top room where he kept his telescope, she would doubtless have left it untouched. But pushed into a damp corner, the bundled object had an air of obscurity, like a parcel left behind in a bus station, forgotten precisely because it was worthless.

She pulled the sheeting aside to reveal two boxes, one atop the other. The bottom one was by far the larger, shaped rather like a child's old-fashioned toy chest, and exquisitely fashioned from a wine-coloured wood. In raised carving on the lid was the letter *M*, formed of delicately overlapping laurel leaves. The smaller box was of serviceable metal, painted a flat black. Neither box was locked. She opened the wooden one first and recoiled when she saw a length of apparently human hair, white-blond and luxuriant. From beneath the fall of hair projected a tiny pair of kidskin boots. A doll, Suzanne presumed, drawing back the sweep of hair to reveal a miniature hand, and then a face, with the poreless translucency of alabaster. The moulding and painting of the facial features were lifelike, yet theatrical. The emerald eyes slanted seductively. The mouth was a scarlet bow. This was no child's toy, she realized. The face was that of a temptress, with a disconcerting "come-hither" look.

She felt suddenly uneasy, as if she had stumbled upon the relics of some secret rite. She found herself irrationally resenting the potent, superior expression of the inanimate creature in the box. She grasped the figure round its middle, her fingers plunging through the thick hair. She realized she wanted to shake loose the power of this thing, as a wilful child would break open a rattle to see what it held. First, she felt the yielding nap of velvet. Then her entire hand was enmeshed in a lattice of strings and finely beaten wire. Pulling the figure from the box, she saw what her fingers had already told her. This green-clad lady was a marionette. The jointed body trembled in Suzanne's hand, then went limp. But the proud head stayed erect, the small, white, sensual face confronting her with a knowing look.

Suzanne lay the puppet full-length on the table, face up, and folded its tiny hands across its chest, so that it lay like a knight's lady in effigy. There, you are quite dead now, she thought, and then immediately caught herself up for having involuntarily entered some kind of child's playtime. Yet, she felt driven to see what else was in the box. Or more properly, who else.

She lifted a layer of old patchwork quilting to reveal a second puppet. This one was a youth with hair of curling auburn silk. He wore a brown cap with a long tassel, a leather jerkin and dove-grey breeches tucked into knee-high boots. Strung across his shoulder was a tiny lute so that Suzanne understood he was probably a minstrel. Unlike the haughty lady, his face was open, impressionably young, like fresh bread on which a stronger will might imprint what it chose. He would be no match for the lady, Suzanne saw, but plummet like a sparrow caught by a hawk. She put him on the other side of the box, away from the temptress, so that he might have some respite.

The third and last marionette (and no wonder, Suzanne thought, that he had been laid deepest) had an aspect so horrific she nearly dropped him. Slits of eyes peered out at her from behind matted hair. The visage verged on cadaverous. Charcoal accentuated the hollow cheeks, the flesh scooped out by some dark inner obsession. Vengeance, Suzanne conjectured, or blood lust. For there were red stains on the puppet's long dark cloak, and the crimson ribbons that streamed from his fingers showed only too graphically how much blood he had spilled. He looked as if he had a lair on the moors. She fancied she could smell the bog. By day, he crept under the great bell of his cape and pressed his face close to the sponge of rotting vegetation. It pleased her to pack him back in his wooden box and cover him again, willing his evil away.

Could the puppets have belonged to one of Murdo's children, she wondered. He had spoken so little of them. She knew their names: Jeremy, Callum, and Clara. "They have their own lives," was Murdo's succinct response when she inquired about them. "They visit about once a year." She understood that he had let them go, and she questioned him no further. His children were adults moving in their own spheres, whom she might or might not meet. Yet here she was fingering puppets that had once been theirs. Perhaps it was because these were not ordinary toys – no ragged-eared Pooh Bears or hard-faced Barbies – that her curiosity was so stirred. These marionettes suggested fiery imaginations, deft fingers, bodily grace, and patience.

She moved next to the smaller metal box and was surprised by her own fumbling when she undid the clasp. Did her awkwardness stem from guilt? Was she indeed violating something best left private?

At first she thought the box was empty. But when she held the interior up toward the oil lamp, a slim manila envelope tumbled out. It was blank and unsealed. She untucked the flap and took out two photographs, black and white snapshots with a worn scalloped edge. Both showed the same young girl with fair chin-length hair. The face was pure Botticelli, Flora of *La Primavera*. A guileless face, as yet absolutely untrammelled by life. What the young woman projected, even in the fading snapshot, was the clear gaze of innocence. In one photo she stood in a long skirt and hip-length cardigan, hands folded in front, with the quiet air of a novice. In the other, she looked down at the baby in her arms. The child, wrapped in a lacy shawl, grasped a strand of the girl's straight, pale hair.

Suzanne heard a discreet cough behind her, and turned to see Murdo standing in the doorway.

"I see," he said, "that you have found Miranda."

Suzanne registered the chill in his tone. The first wife. So she had indeed been prying.

"I haven't seen these for many years," he said, taking the photos from her.

"And little Jeremy, too," he said, studying the photo with the baby. "Who would have thought such a bonny little boy would grow up into my hair-shirted son? He's probably in the former Yugoslavia right now, ducking bullets, or mopping up the blood of the wounded with his Greenpeace T-shirt. Or skulking through Cambodia, snuffling up the ordures of Pol Pot. He has a penchant for suffering, has Jeremy."

Murdo snorted. It was an ugly sound, Suzanne thought. She had never before heard him be so derisive. Her discovery was beginning to take on the uncomfortable grittiness of a bad dream. Do not, under any circumstances, open the box.

"Murdo," she started, uncertain where to go next. What *had* she opened? Then: "I had no idea that I was treading on something so personal."

"Personal? Personal!" He made the word sound distasteful, and his face in the lamplight was one she did not recognize – gloomy, older, embittered.

"These were Miranda's." He gestured towards the marionettes. "She had the most beautiful hands. And quick. Like white birds. She made these wooden things live. She'd keep a group of snotty-nosed children in the village hall captivated for an hour and more. She had a voice too, like silver bells."

"That's the Queen of Elfland," he said, pointing to the green-clad lady. "And that one's True Thomas the Rhymer, poor chap. And that," he peered into the box, "is Long Lankin, murderer of the moors. Miranda loved the old ballads. She was a descendant of Sir Walter Scott. Did I tell you that?"

"No," she answered. "You've told me very little."

"Ah," he said. "Well." Then shook himself, like a large dog coming in from the wet.

"Look, my dear Suz. I came to tell you that I'm off to London for a few days. Postgraduate student in a bit of a mess, I'm afraid. Must just go and hold his hand for a bit. History of bungled suicide. That sort of thing. But brilliant boy. Brilliant."

"You've got the Land Rover if you need to go to the city," he added. "I really must get off. See you soon, then."

And he was gone, without even the touch of his hand on her shoulder.

When she got to the house, she noticed the two gouges in the gravel of the circular driveway. Murdo had apparently spun the tires in his hurry to get away.

She was shocked at how relieved she was that he had gone.

5

Beware of Lambs

The confrontation with Murdo, if indeed it had been that, left her unsettled. It was the first time she had genuinely welcomed his absence. Yet as the afternoon wore on, she found this was not an unqualified relief.

She supposed she was upset because she had blundered rather badly. She had been presumptuous, she thought, to open the box like an inquisitive and naive Pandora. The image of the puppet with its haunted face and bloody cloak sprang again to mind. She had opened the damned box and out had come, not evil – but remnants of Murdo's past. The first wife with her child-pure features and gracile body. A young wife who had died young. How or of what, Suzanne did not yet know. There was only the fact. Twice widowed. A blow of fate that set Murdo apart from other men. At their very first meeting, she had recognized immediately the signs of suffering on his face. Ada would have said: "That one has been through the vale of soul-making."

Murdo had been through that vale, and then through again. Suzanne had perceived in him no rancour; not even the stoic resignation that is so often just a mask for despair. Rather she had sensed a courageous acceptance so profound as to border on mystery. Here, she thought, was a man who had transcended the quotidian and tawdry by going through the full agony of loss. He had accomplished this, purged of hatred and raw anger.

So she had believed until this afternoon. For Murdo's cynicism, particularly about his son Jeremy, struck her as quite vile.

Suzanne abhorred cynicism. *Cynos* was Greek for dog, was it not? She had never understood the connection, unless it had to do with limited vision and a predilection for rolling in the muck. Yet thinking back, Suzanne wondered how genuine Murdo's negativity had been. His remarks about Jeremy might well have been a defence thrown up to deflect his anger at her. She had unwittingly pried into his past after all, although she could not understand how such treasured objects had come to be left in a mouldering outbuilding.

A particularly unpleasant possibility occurred to her, one in which she immediately felt herself to be implicated. What if it was Murdo's second wife who had put the two boxes there, well away from the house itself? What if it was jealousy that had prompted her, a desire to wipe her predecessor out? And so she had gone through the house, room by room, exorcising the first wife's presence. Suzanne had heard of women doing such things, making a bonfire in the backyard and putting to the flame everything that remained of the woman who preceded them: letters, journals, clothing, photographs. Or they might, as appeared the case here, simply store them away out of sight.

Kirstie. That was the second wife. A very Scottish, muscular name. Kirstie. Had Kirstie been jealous of Miranda? Was it an absurdity to be jealous of the dead? Suzanne thought not, especially where the grounds were possessive passion. The absurdity was in assuming that by destroying the dead's belongings, you extinguished their power. From Ada she had learned to accept the persistence of the spirit after death as a given. "Nothing is ever destroyed, Suzanne. Transformed, yes.

Remember, we have the stars within us, and their energy is eternal."

Ada conversed with the dead. This was not, Suzanne discovered early on, a maternal talent to be bruited abroad. Not at all on a par with pie making or proficiency at bridge. At eight years of age, Suzanne had had her face smacked sharply by a teacher to whom she had babbled blithely of Ada's midnight colloquies with ghosts. Was it then Ada had first counselled her on the wisdom of silence and the dense potency of the secret?

Outside the house, therefore, Suzanne learned never to speak of her mother's spiritual companions. Inside, she came to see these ethereal visitors as an integral part of the household.

Suzanne never saw these spirits with whom her mother spoke. Nor did she actually hear their conversations. At most, she might catch a reverberation, not unlike the swell and dip of sea surge. She was never afraid because Ada assured her all the visitors were benign. No evil force could penetrate the hermetic enclosure that Ada had created from their clapboard house. She had purified the rooms with salt and set up her own invisible watchtowers. Suzanne believed in this fastness her mother had made.

She did not believe she had inherited her mother's powers. Or if she had, she had no inkling of them. By osmosis perhaps, she had absorbed Ada's habit of compassionate empathy. It was this talent, Suzanne believed, that enabled her to look out of the eyes of women long dead – the Magdalenes, the maidens and the witches. This was not an automatic or a painless process, and it seemed to encompass something more than just imaginative projection. Sometimes, after many hours of silent communing with these women whose images she studied, Suzanne would find herself tugged by an irresistible urge for sleep. When she woke, usually at dusk, she would catch the faintest echo of murmuring voices. Never yet had she experienced anything that made her afraid. Although she was of course apprehensive about the work to come – the inescapable emotional confrontation with witch prickers and the cruel burnings.

Now, for the first time, she had come across an image of a woman long dead that caused her a deep visceral unease. She speculated that this reaction might be an emotional contagion. If she was right, and it was Kirstie who had put the box out in the ancient barn, she might well have been contaminated by the woman's envy or even hatred of Miranda. Even as she thought this, Suzanne realized she was dissembling. This jealousy she felt was not absorbed second-hand, but was peculiarly her own. She was ashamed. To be jealous of a dead woman was worse than unworthy. It was despicable. Suzanne made herself relive the moment of looking at the photograph. Seeing Miranda's virginal face and form had been a profound shock. Was it the girl's youth that prompted this envy? That tender, unlined state in which Miranda was now locked forever. Suzanne knew Miranda's skin had been flawless, even given the faded tones of the old snapshot. Her natural scent would be of violets. Whereas she herself was sometimes rank with the smell of sex, or menstrual blood, or sweat.

Stop these ludicrous comparisons, she told herself. Quite out of character, she felt herself teetering at the top of a perilous slide. At the bottom were ignominy and self-doubt. Again, she seemed to sense the presence of an external force that did indeed want to topple her down that precipitous chute. The image of the veil returned to her, the floating whiteness that had haunted her briefly in Amsterdam. Miranda's? Kirstie's? Two young brides.

At thirty-four, Suzanne knew she had already lost the pure translucency of youth. She had begun to wonder if it was the accumulation of experience itself that rendered the skin opaque. Rationally, she knew she was still attractive, tall, slim, and strong. The word people most often used to describe her appearance was exotic, for from her mother she had inherited the high, wide cheekbones, full lips, and upward slanting eyes of Romany ancestors. Her eyes were her best feature: virtually black, the iris surprisingly ringed with purple. For years, she had worn her hair in the same style, absolutely straight, chin-length and with a central part. In profile, with her slightly beaked nose, she resembled certain portraits of Nefertiti.

The contrast with the young woman in the photograph could not have been more marked. Dark drama as opposed to fair delicacy. Sensual (Suzanne knew that this was what she projected) against maidenly. All that she and Miranda had in common was slenderness.

She and Miranda. She and Kirstie. Miranda, Kirstie and Suzanne. The realization hit her as forcibly as a slap. Which was, she thought, exactly what she deserved for this astounding omission. Here she was, Suzanne Clelland, self-defined feminist, a writer bound in with the lives of women, past and present. And yet until now, she had not fully recognized the reality of the two women who had preceded her as Murdo's wives. How could she have been so incurious? And if they had both still been alive? Would she have questioned Murdo about their appearance, character, talents? Suzanne thought not, principally because she saw her union with Murdo as so very idiosyncratic. As if the sun and moon had come together to make a planet entirely new, with a heat that subsumed the raggedness of their respective pasts.

Besides, she had always intensely disliked the pillow talk ritual of documenting former lovers. Such revelations seemed to her a kind of sickly smug voyeurism. She would squirm away, rather than listen to the most tellingly intimate secrets of people she had never met. So it was certainly not that she wanted to broach Murdo on his return, asking for detailed accounts of his life with Miranda and with Kirstie. It was only that she required some meagre idea of the two

women, a way to picture them. Until her discovery of the
boxes in the barn, they had been only abstractions, wispy
clouds woven into Murdo's circlet of pain.

Now their histories, their habitation of this stone house,
were suddenly palpable. She felt their lives as a literal weight.
For a moment, she went dizzy and had to grasp on to the
newel post at the bottom of the stair. The wooden knob in
her hand felt strangely warm as though it still held both
women's bodily heat. The knob would have pressed into
their palms – both Miranda's and Kirstie's – as they made
their way up the stairs at night, weary and heavy with child.
Or perhaps they had clung to the post with both hands,
pressed their foreheads to the wood, and wept.

As she pictured this, Suzanne became aware of an
extraordinary odour; or rather, a succession of smells, each
with its own distinctly pungent assault. First, there was the
sweet yeastiness of rising bread; she was sure she could detect
oatmeal and honey. Then came a waft of a woman's perfume,
darkly fruity, almost overwhelming. Last there was an
unpleasant whiff associated with a badly ventilated toilet, or
a stopped drain perhaps, or a baby's diaper left to soak in a
washtub. These separate odours then mingled, and the atmosphere of the sprawling house was absolutely transformed.
Suzanne understood that what she could smell was the past;
the matchless perfume of the family unit.

As a young girl, visiting the houses of friends, she had
always been struck how each family made its own peculiar
broth of smells distinct as a genetic marker. It was a phenomenon Suzanne was ever after to associate with what she
thought of as "classical" families; that is, those with a father,
even an absent father, and with more than one child. She
could not honestly ever remember envying these households
with their powerfully idiosyncratic odours, particularly if
there was a strident undercurrent of sweat or blood from a
hunting jacket. These potent domestic broths seemed to her

a little unsavoury after the rarefied atmosphere of Ada's abundant drying herbs. There had been a bracing cleanliness about the smell of their home, neither chemical nor detergent, but as if Ada had conspired to bring the most pleasing scents of the vegetable world inside.

The odours that surrounded Suzanne now were not at all pleasing. She was seized by a terrible anxiety. It was as if the house itself were trying to spit her out one of its cruciform windows. The sensation was electric and singularly unpleasant. She had an irrational urge to fight back; to roam through every single room, delve into every cupboard, nook and alcove. She wondered if through this wandering, she might succeed in making peace with the place. For in the month she had spent here, she had to admit that she was still at odds with Murdo's ancestral home. Sometimes she thought it was the heaviness of the stone itself that oppressed her. Or perhaps it was the blatant waste of its empty rooms that disturbed her, while outside thousands roamed the roads, sleeping in viaducts or under bridges.

In London, she had rented a single room, in the house belonging to her friend Gemma. The walls were gleaming white, and the wide window overlooked the Thames where bright barges bobbed at their moorings. The boats' bold paintwork, crimson, midnight blue, tangerine, reminded Suzanne of Gypsy caravans, and therefore of her mother.

When she learned of her mother's death, which had been totally unexpected, Suzanne for some weeks experienced the loss as an excruciating bodily pain. An animal with razor teeth gnawed at her heart.

Twice, that same ferret-like creature had eaten away at Murdo's heart. Here. In this house. And his pain must have spilled out, she thought, and been absorbed by the walls. And what of Miranda's and Kirstie's pain? Was their residual anguish the source of her agitation? Or were their spirits indeed still here, reinforcing this idea of herself as interloper?

The dead, as Suzanne knew well, were often larger and more potent than in life. Kirstie and Miranda had a mythic power that she could never undo. Although she was still loath to question Murdo directly about his first two wives, how else was she to know anything of them? If she did not soon have some sense of them as individuals, she feared dire consequences. Yet what these might be, she had no idea.

Even as she formed this thought, she was aware of a trickle of wetness down her inner thigh and that familiar heaviness in her lower abdomen. She was a week early, which perhaps accounted for her extreme sensitivity to the atmosphere of the house with Murdo gone. She remembered then she had very few tampons left, and decided to walk to the local village shop, rather than drive. The four miles there and back would help her relax and ease the already noticeable cramps.

Surprisingly, the shop had a copy of *The Guardian*, which she purchased along with an outrageously overpriced box of tampons. Serving behind the counter were two elderly women, alike enough to be twins. Or perhaps they deliberately tried to resemble one another, Suzanne thought, with their identical harlequin spectacles, flowered aprons and fine white hair so tightly permed that the pale pink of their scalps was visible. She paid and was about to pick up her purchases when one of the women produced a brown paper bag that she flapped in the air. "You'll be wanting to put your box in this," she said. Her look was stern, her remark more command than suggestion. Suzanne deferred, rather than transgress the norms and offend the woman's sensibilities. She had foolishly forgotten that this was rural Scotland. The fact that women bleed must be hidden.

Just as she was going out the door, she heard one woman address the other in an undertone. At first the words made no sense. Suzanne was not yet accustomed to the local accent, but she had found that by silently repeating to herself what she heard, syllable by syllable, she could eventually unravel the meaning. As she came level with the "Beware of Lambs" sign on the road home, the shopkeeper's words fell abruptly into place. "That Napier's a devil. He ruined that young girl's life."

She had to clutch at the wooden sign as her uterus contracted in a fiery pang, threatening to double her over.

6

Gemma

Gemma Tithe was plucking a chicken, while belting out "The Battle Hymn of the Republic." The song's rousing vigour imposed a rhythm on the tedious work. Later, after showering, she would have to use a pick comb to remove the white tendrils that clung to her hair and eyebrows.

She left the words of the song unchanged. She was content enough that it was the Lord who was coming, His truth, His victory and His damned grapes of wrath being trod. Like most Christian hymns, it was an intrinsically male song, a paean to violence and conflict. "His terrible swift sword" was not unlike the cleaver with which she would later behead the chickens and slice through the purplish gristle of their rubbery legs. She loathed the whole disgusting business, and the Battle Hymn was thus the perfect accompaniment. The chorus primed her energy. For every "Glory! Glory! Hallelujah!" she could extract a fistful of feathers. Like that other fistful, she thought. Another lean, holstered man, wreaking His vengeance, bringing His truth, His law. Glory! Glory! Hallelujah! Gemma sang.

Her voice was supple still, arcing like swift water. "Like a doe skin," her grade school teacher on the island had told her mother. Who had radiated such pride at the telling, Gemma had felt the whole shape of her mother's hand outlined in heat on her shoulders. An invisible shawl, Gemma thought in years afterwards, made of her mother's blood, heat, and love. She could in times of dire stress and trouble, summon the sensation, the very imprint of her mother's hands, the warmth worn lightly as a blessing, purifying as wood smoke. She had this in common with Suzanne, a rare continuance of the mother's presence long after the woman herself had passed on. But passed on where? For she shared with Suzanne too, a perplexing mystery at the heart of their loss. Both their mothers had disappeared near water, leaving behind a bundle of possessions on shore. Suzanne's mother had left a pair of silver earrings and an embroidered shawl tucked in a crevice on the rocky shore of Cape Breton. As well, there was a note to her daughter, which Suzanne kept with her always, its folds gone soft as linen.

Gemma's mother had, they supposed, swum or walked out into the Caribbean Sea. Gemma pictured her mother moving slowly, a stately swaying of hips and breasts through that quiet blue. Much as she had moved through her life, unhurried, dignified, bearing her responsibilities with such grace and lightness, it was as if she glided through water. She created her own element, radiated her own power, which could temper the pain of so many others, and not simply her own children.

Rolled in a bundle on the white sands, she had left behind her "festival" skirt, trumpeting scarlet flowers against emerald green, and her pair of clacking bones. These were gazelle bones, or so Gemma had been led to believe, brought generations ago from Africa. Her mother had used the bones to make music when she sang. The bones played best under a full moon. They were more sprightly then, Gemma's mother said. Her song was a low, throaty hum. The bones performed their bright staccato. Gemma's sister Leah had those bones now, played them under the island moon.

When Gemma last went back to the island, Leah told her the bones were always warm to the touch. They too, held her mother's life heat. A heat that Gemma could will to spread about her shoulders, through sheer force of remembrance and desire.

So often now she found she needed to summon the invisible shawl that was her mother's presence. When she comforted a woman whose nostrils had been torn open by a man in a rage. When she stopped toddlers in the park from popping used condoms in their mouths, plucked from a ground that was more litter than grass. When paper bags of excrement and worms were pushed through the mail slot of the refuge. When a man in the first stages of AIDS, marked out by the fact he lived in special Council housing, was clubbed at a bus stop. The assailants had been swaddled in layers of clothing and wore thick rubber masks and gloves. When she herself received death threats, by letter or by telephone, from skinheads who aligned themselves with the National Front or the British National Party or the Movement for a Racially Pure Britain. Or from the deranged husband of one of the hundreds of women who each year sought safety at the shelter.

She wanted her mother's heat and love suffusing her skin when she looked at the city and saw Armageddon. When Gemma first arrived in London at the age of fourteen, the city seemed to her cold, dirty, and hostile. Twenty years later, she looked back on those initial impressions as though on a golden age. For in two decades, the small scattered pockets of prejudice, hatred, and greed had festered and spread, just as had the cardboard cities, diseases old and new, child prostitution, and violence. The most terrible irony was that a woman had set this poison in motion, although Gemma had so often found it difficult to grasp that the grocer's daughter was a woman. Gone from power now and made a Baroness, but with the same static, moulded hair, the same narrow pinched mouth opening and closing like the rigid clasp of her

omnipresent handbag. Greed had done it, had ultimately
made this city something you might glimpse through the
gates of hell.

Recently, Gemma had dreamt of a great flood, the water
rising steadily up the steps of the British Museum and the
National Portrait Gallery, snaking its way through the chan-
cel of St. Martin-in-the-Fields. Everywhere the rising flood
displaced the people who huddled and bedded down in
doorways. This was no purifying flood, no washing away of
pain and pestilence. In the dream, she saw the grey waters
freeze, gritty peaked waves frozen all over the city, as though
a new ice age had come.

So in her worst moments, Gemma saw the city as
through hell fire, flood, and grim, heart-locking ice. Some
nights, she would sit on the edge of her bed and weep. This
most often happened after ten straight hours of cradling hurt
women and bruised children, trying to instil hope in those
who believed they could bear life no longer, coping with dissension in the kitchen and final notices from the Electricity
Board, of going cap in hand (Gemma did not in fact wear a
cap, but a sleek black matador's hat that was one of her few
prized possessions) to the local grocers, charities, and to the
Council, always the damned Council. Certain nights, it was
all she could do not to sit and howl like an animal. The tales
she heard were sometimes too much to bear. Just as were the
most vile of the death threat letters with their recipes for dis-
membering "stunted black dykes."

Gemma was a short, black lesbian. As she saw it, this
meant she was three-times blessed. She was not disadvan-
taged and certainly no victim. She rejoiced in the fact she
had been born black, compact of form and, above all, female.
It was women who redeemed the world from horror. She
had been fully aware of this fact for at least twenty years;
unconsciously, she thought she had probably absorbed it at
her mother's breast.

For Gemma, there was quite simply nothing in the world like the laughter of women. In a room where their laughter spilled out (like silver, bubbling water, she thought) and was caught up and spun round, touching everyone in a sublime contagion, then it was heaven. This laughter of women was purest song, and here, Gemma was at home.

She had not been at home on the island when she returned. She had first escaped (or so she saw it now; at fourteen she had seen herself as exiled) because of a scholarship won through her efforts and her mother's indefatigable support. Her mother had wanted Gemma, the youngest of her daughters, to go free. For except by escape through an unfettered sailing of the spirit, the life of all women on the island was one of service – to men and to the children men put in them. Rum, bananas, cocoa, sugar. That was the island, with most men indulging copiously in the rum. They drank and preened, announced themselves to be macho men, and then strove to embody the image. When Gemma had gone back at age fifteen, her own father had been so drunk he had not recognized her. She went to speak with him, where he stood jawing with his cronies, and he did not recognize her. He put out his hand and pawed her breasts, and she was sickened and disgusted by him.

Of course, he then no longer lived with Gemma's mother; had not, in fact, since Gemma was four. And a very good thing too, Gemma thought, as she marched away from him forever. This she considered a very posh British expression, one she had learned at school. She had soon had the accent down to a t, effortlessly mimicking the upper-class girls, their swank and snootiness and pet phrases. While their attempts to take off her island lilt were all dismal. And a very good thing, too. You said this with the mouth a little pursed, nose in the air, and perhaps the tiniest flounce of the pleated skirt of your school uniform. The phrase and the nose in the air served her very well indeed the day she turned her back on her drunken lout of a father. That day too, she had turned her back on the idea of the island as home, although she had not fully realized it at the time.

Home was the bosom of her mother, her mother's laughter, and her mother's songs. Home was the companionship of her sisters and of all the women on the island, a silky warm companionship, easy and unquestioning, where you are borne up on the spring of that rising laughter, that particular silvery laughter of women, only women, together.

At her London school, Gemma found such companionship first with the black scholarship girls from Hackney and Brixton. They shared Gemma's quickness and her fire. As a group, they were admired for their daring. They were fearless in vaulting the school wall and breaking bounds without getting caught. Yet academically, few could touch them.

By her third year, Gemma had made many firm friends, young women who were brown, pink, olive, and chalk-white. To this day, she detested phrases like "women of colour;" indeed, most of the jargon of the politically correct movement. She described herself as black because black was what she was. And inevitably she had fallen out with women who were angered at her refusal to align herself with "radical lesbians of colour."

Which would have meant repudiating women like her friend Suzanne, who admittedly had done a remarkably stupid thing by marrying. Unlike many of their acquaintances, Gemma did not see Suzanne's marriage as a deliberate act of apostasy, but rather as heedless folly. She was certain Suzanne had been seduced by a false image. Gemma had seen Murdo Napier at a distance (she could not have borne any closer proximity) and had pegged him immediately. The ever-so-slight stoop, suggesting burdens disproportionate for a man of his stature and class. The furrowed brow, the enigmatic, melancholy mouth. Above all, the mournful eyes, where the pupil appears to have no depth at all because it has been flattened by pain. Suffering, Tragic Man. In Murdo's case, suffering, tragic widower. Such was the false image that had sucked in Suzanne. And how often had Gemma seen this story played out to its end, with its inevitable reversal of roles for the women taken in.

Murdo had quite a massive head, Gemma recalled, and Suzanne had seemed much taken with his so-called brilliance. Well, she thought, clutching another fistful of feathers, men were good at games. There were instants (mere instants only) when she could feel quite sorry for them; their worlds were so highly ritualized, so shallow. She listened to them sometimes in pubs – the mates, the chums, the buds, the old boys – and heard them speak their lines as if they had learned them by rote from a book written centuries before. They joked around. They played tricks on one another.

They liked one-upmanship. They liked to win. It seemed to Gemma that they were always engaged in some kind of war.

By and large, she did not care for men. With few exceptions, she preferred that no male over the age of ten enter her home.

She missed Suzanne terribly and hoped fervently her misalliance would meet with a speedy and relatively painless end. It was such a waste. Murdo would entice Suzanne up to suffer with him on his cross, and then, hey-presto, he'd slip down and leave her pinned there. Oh, come home, Suzanne.

Gemma counted the naked plucked corpses. Eight down and still two to go. She must get them into the freezer tonight. They're country-fresh, the local poulterer told her when offering the birds. Gemma hoped the poor bastards had been free-ranging; not nailed to a board and shot through with growth hormones.

Brutality was pervasive. Last week she had taken to hospital a woman whose husband had inserted a wire coathanger through her cheek and dragged her across the kitchen.

In front of the children. The week before that, she had counselled a woman who had had her face pushed down over a
lit gas jet. And before that. And before that. Which was why
Gemma maintained instruction in the art of self-defence
should be mandatory for every schoolgirl in the country.

Not to attack. Although she herself had sometimes to
fight off the blind instinctual urge for vengeance. "The master's tools will never dismantle the master's house." So said
Audre Lorde. And so Gemma repeated to herself daily, to
help quell her fury.

Gemma was weary. She decided to seal each of the
chickens in a plastic bag and store them in the fridge for the
night. Tomorrow, she would tackle the gutting. She would
ask Marcia and some of the others to help.

She felt a stab of pity for the dead birds lying naked in
their bags, even though she personally disliked the taste of
chicken. This aversion dated back to her first British Airways
flight when she left her island home. The stewardess had presented her with the plastic dinner tray, tidily divided into its
little segments of main course, salad and desert. The main
course was a particularly pallid piece of chicken dotted with
peas. What most confused her was not the plastic presenta-
tion, but the cutlery rolled in a paper napkin. Until that day,
she had always eaten with her hands, most often taking a bit
of baked yam, and fish, wrapping them in a palm leaf, and
then eating alone under the shade of a favourite tree. On the
island, one ate with one's hands. Metal implements did not
come into it. None of her reading on the island – neither Sir
Walter Scott, nor Virginia Woolf, nor even Iris Murdoch had
prepared Gemma for the knife and spoon (both recognizable
as cooking utensils) and the two (why two?) pronged devices
she found nestled in the paper napkin.

But she was always a quick study, and glancing across the
aisle, she noted how the white tourist couple wielded their
cutlery. Perhaps, she reflected, putting the last of chickens

away, that incident had marked her real initiation to the culture of the Mother Country (what a misnomer!). It had all begun then with the lifting of the knife and the larger pronged tool, the spearing and the cutting and the lifting of food to the lips. Mastering this process of eating with the help of metal implements was the first of a series of adaptations at which Gemma was to prove herself superb.

On the plane, she had hidden well just how thoroughly she was perplexed by the ways of her new homeland. She had had her first glimmerings then of how disjunct her past and future were. The island she had left behind, and the London in which she arrived, were as different one from the other as her island must have seemed to her African ancestors. History had spared her their degradation and pain. What they bequeathed her were courage and a persistence of spirit; and a warmth that still haunted the clacking bones.

And so she had adapted to this city, so often shrouded in grey weather; to the blasts of hot, stale air in the underground; to climbing into damp, clammy sheets winter and summer; to the regulation school underpants (knickers, they called them) of cotton flannel so thick they would stand erect on a bed or dresser top if you balanced them carefully. And much later, as a young woman free of the strictures of boarding school, she had learned to adapt to the unsolicited attentiveness of the London constabulary. If you were black, you were stopped and questioned far more often than were the city's paler citizens. Racism, Gemma came to understand, was part of the policeman's armature.

But London had its compensations. She loved the river. Tonight, when she got home, she would sit a while in the bay window of her second-floor bedroom, and watch the full moon shatter and reassemble again in the gentle friction of the water. The bones, she recalled, played best under a full moon.

Gemma conjured up the heat of her mother's hands, and the picture of the sprightly white bones. And she thought

again, as she so often did, of the absurdity that was the source
of women's laughter. In time, every woman born came to
this tacit recognition; that history had played on them a cruel
joke of cosmic proportions, and implications. Somewhere
along the line, a millennium ago, the balance had been
thrown off and the humans with penises declared themselves
the centre of creation. The consequences of this skewing of
power were so wrong, so inept (to put the kindest face on
it), that women had no choice but to laugh when they could.
Laughter was the answer to this profound absurdity with
which history presented them. And the beauty of the absurd
was that it held the promise of its opposite. So that the laughter of women was also solace and a manifest hope. And I rise
up on that bosom of laughter, thought Gemma. I am at
home there.

Oh, come home, Suzanne.

7

Murdo

There were times Murdo feared his brain might burst, a possibility that greatly offended his innate fastidiousness. As a young man, he had been obsessed by his chosen discipline. But why not call his subject what it was? A ravening madness, a seductive, twisting Whore who shook him awake in the middle of the night, his stomach curdling, his head a hollow gourd in which She (the Whore) beat a gong in dinning repetition, the better, She told him, to sound out infinity. He would slide out of bed, try to escape Her, place his throbbing forehead against the cold of the windowpane, his eyes shut fast against the mocking vastness of Night; and worse, those twinkling tormentors, the stars, each prick of light a needle through his already riddled brain.

Once, he had come close to worshipping those stars in their majestic courses. The sovereign galaxies exalted him as he lay all night in his narrow astronomer's coffin, separated from the damp and teeming terrestrial world, the hooting owls, the slinking ferrets and scrabbling foxes all left quite behind. He believed then (did he not?) that he experienced a sublime transportation (what the inane chatterers of today would call an out-of-body experience, or more fatuously still, an OBE). He had tasted the shimmering reaches of the

Milky Way (licking silver from his lips), felt his blood beat at the same frequency as the pulsar, the "powerhouse," at the centre of Crab Nebula. He had been drunk (yes, he must admit it) on the dream of unlocking the ultimate secret, the one seamless overarching theorem that explained every residual mystery, from gravitation to the very structure of matter, including his own flesh, and the flesh of his three wives. From the radiant dust of the farthest reaches of the universe to a single cell in his thumbnail, this "theory of everything" had been his Grail. He had seen himself as one of the outriders of the cosmos, in service of his Mistress, Mathematics, and her Consort, Physics.

Simply recalling this sickly romanticized attempt at self-creation, this puerile folly, caused him considerable chagrin. And heartburn. Outrider of the cosmos, indeed. Bad enough even in the days of his youth, but now such images had been cheapened and trivialized by those film epics of "outer space," populated by creatures with misshapen heads, and muscular men and nubile women cavorting in spandex pyjamas. Callum had been besotted with those nonsensical films for a time. Appallingly bad taste came naturally to the boy. Murdo could remember a toothbrush which Callum had set in pride of place in the bracket beneath the bathroom cabinet. Oversized, dull black, the words *Darth Vader* embossed on the handle, along with some obscene visage glowering out of the plastic. Confronting that object in the mornings had become more than he could stomach, and Murdo had eventually flung the wretched thing into the middle of a clump of stinging nettles.

How the boy had managed to locate it, Murdo never knew. Callum had, on very rare occasion, demonstrated a remarkable sixth sense – nature's compensation, perhaps, for his lack of verbal skills. The boy had plunged into the bush, extracted his toothbrush, and emerged with face, bare arms and legs all finely cross-hatched in bright red. He had not winced or whimpered, despite the stinging rash. But rather than admire the boy's fortitude, Murdo found his son's forbearance unsettling, even uncanny. Callum was how old then – six, eight? A normal child would at least have moaned a little. That incident, and many others to come, fed Murdo's fancy that Callum was actually a changeling, some elves' progeny left in place of his real child. Given Callum's frequently bizarre behaviour, Murdo sometimes found this admittedly ridiculous notion profoundly comforting.

Then too, from his first glimmerings of self-consciousness, Callum had cultivated a deliberately beguiling way with women. He would roll his huge blue eyes upwards and pull a kind of mooning face that Murdo found frankly disgusting. But for reasons Murdo could never fathom, women doted on the boy's antics and fatuous facial expressions. Two of them had fussed over Callum that day he had dragged himself tight-lipped out of the nettles. Nanny Oliphant was it then? And dear old Cook, dabbing calamine lotion on his scratches, popping barley sugar into his greedy open mouth. And while they clucked and cosseted and hung about him in adoring postures, Callum rolled his eyes heavenward, reminding Murdo of those badly executed portraits of saints in ecstasy, who appear to have been very recently goosed.

Yes, the child had had two functioning eyes then. Now, he was asymmetrical, in terms of his organs of vision. And with a nature like Callum's, asymmetry must be the inevitable outcome. Murdo in no way blamed himself for the boy's accident. Callum was a fool, and fools must come to grief. Besides, it was only an eye the boy had lost. Tissue, muscle, fluid. What was the loss of an eye compared with the bitterness of the failed Quest? It had all gone now, the animating vigour, the quickened pulse, the powerhouse behind the search that generated life's meaning. The certainty that he would now never find the exquisite equation that underwrote the mysteries of the world, had rendered him not

simply bitter, but pulped. At his most dejected, he did sometimes see himself as an aging piece of fruit, its inside scooped
right out, its flesh spotted and withered. So, pulped. Or
sometimes, like a piece of wood, riddled with (that word
again) wormholes.

Wormholes were of course, symptomatic of his problem,
of his cumulative failure at, and in life. Ironically, these same
wormholes were staples of the science fiction that had so fascinated the young Callum. And might still for all Murdo
knew, if the drugs in which his son indulged had not by now
destroyed what little brain he had. Could Callum still read?
Could he even – by the most liberal definition – reason?
With Callum this was impossible to judge, based on external
evidence. For in Murdo's presence at least, Callum persisted
in his maddening babble, which was not quite baby-talk, but
some language, or simply strings of sound, of his own invention.

So it struck Murdo as a peculiar double irony that the
ruination of his Quest lay in that absurd, fictitious world of
Callum's boyhood. Fifteen years ago, Murdo had jeered at
Callum's babble of wormholes, of tunnels through the fabric
of time-space, and of a world in ten dimensions (it was simply that we did not have organs to perceive the other six).
Now these concepts were standard for the whizz-bang boys
of theoretical physics. Pumping out their tomes, with their
requisite reams of equations, the superstrings that made a
mockery of his own search for a unified field theory. He had
been left behind. Or rather, he was grossly out of step in a
world where, daily, theory propagated new theory, where
there were now more than 200 types of subatomic particles
(many of them artificially created). The latest, he read, were
wimps (an acronym of sorts for weakly interacting subatomic
particles). The very names themselves, like *superstring* for
example, were detestable. So vulgar, so very American, so
cunningly aimed at the popular market. As in superburger,

supermodel. Super had been one of the few words Callum could actually articulate as a child, usually whilst he stood on his head, and in that dinning repetition children use to drive adults mad.

Murdo did sometimes reflect on the unfairness of identifying his own life's failure with Callum. He recognized that he had troubled relationships with all three of his children. Clara was the only one who sometimes showed him a meagre affection. He had come to dread their annual visits, regarding them as trials he must endure. The problem was not that they challenged him, or subjected him to a flailing criticism. Rather, they ignored him in so far as they could. Jeremy was smoothly supercilious, the exemplum of the cosmopolitan man who has forged his identity everywhere but at home. Clara habitually graced him with a close-lipped smile. Which was actually no comfort as her expression seemed a ghostly mirroring of the look he imagined her mother bravely put on in her last moments. And then there was Callum, who after a year away, would strike Murdo more forcibly than ever as an aberration, an abomination, a monster. Walking the ridgepole, swinging at the end of a rope he had looped round the tower top, babbling, polyvalent, turning up in disguise, never, never still. Or when still, having the appearance of one dead, and if you touched him on the shoulder, he would topple to the floor in a fit. Disgusting, maddening Callum, as unruly and unpredictable as this wilful universe now postulated by contemporary physics. Turbulent disorder, ever-thickening complexity, and the organizing principle emerging suddenly at the very edge of chaos. This all recalled for Murdo Callum's inane gabbling, which would culminate abruptly in a word, or series of words, that seemed to have both sense and resonance. No doubt Callum, in his heedless drug taking, could glimpse those six other dimensions that lie perpendicular to our own, secreted inside the superstrings.

I am too old for all this, thought Murdo. His own goal was now antiquated, forever outpaced by the proliferating theories of the whizz-bang boys. His quest was driven by the desire for an elegant simplicity, the perfect yoking of quantum mechanics and gravitational curvature of space, a final equation in which the paradoxes of Bohr, Dirac, and even Gödel were all subsumed. Like a pack of wolves, he used to think, lying peacefully down together. No wars, but a wondrous consonance. All quite gone now, he thought. No possibility of the unified field, that "theory of everything." Not now that the whizz-bang boys had unlocked their numerous Pandora's boxes at the very heart of the universe.

Sometimes, he found himself wishing he had been born in the days of Newton, and able to luxuriate in the certainties of the clockwork universe, where bodies could indeed attract and repel each other over distance, and space was merely emptiness.

How the young man he had been would have despised the failed old man he had become. Over the years, Murdo had lost the ability to weep. But if he had it still, he would have wept for that young man in his wooden coffin, his bright eyes, his firm flesh, his heart (yes, his heart) open to glories cosmic and sidereal. What an innocent he had been. When was that? The wooden coffin on the hill in Hampshire? He calculated rapidly. He must have been seventeen. Now forty-five years had passed. Forty-five years of incremental loss, confusion, doubt, and embitterment.

Once, he had been as naive as Suzanne, something he would naturally never tell her. He found her dedication to her work endearing. She was so terribly certain that her scribblings would make a difference. Poring over her pictures, a pencil tucked behind one ear, its vector-like tip emerging like a pure sign from the curve of her ebony hair. When she studied her engravings and reproductions, her brow a little wrinkled, Suzanne seemed to him endearingly childlike, much like Clara when she had played at dressing her dolls. He knew Suzanne would be outraged by such comparisons (in fact, it amused and even aroused him, to think just how outraged.) But of course he would never reveal to her that he regarded her work as fatuous. No more than he would comment on her rather risible background. From his earliest school days, he had been trained in taciturnity and in keeping his own counsel. Earlier even than that, at the hands of his father. Holding his tongue, silencing his real opinion, was as ingrained in him as the habits of cleanliness, regular evacuation of the bowels, the taking of air and exercise.

He wanted to keep Suzanne. She had a natural intelligence, if somewhat woefully applied. She was not a chatterer, and she respected his privacy. Uppermost, her body inflamed his desire as no woman's had since Kirstie. There was something in the combination of the long balletic legs, with the fullness of breasts and hips, that consistently aroused him. Even thinking of her, here in the train, he could feel his erection, so that he had to lay his newspaper open over his lap, and stare out the window as if deep in thought. Deep in her. Perhaps because of her North American upbringing, she was far less inhibited than most of the women he had known, except when he had paid for highly specialized services. Suzanne enjoyed, even encouraged, physical positions he had assumed a feminist would consider demeaning. And he had to admit that her politics, her highly charged notion of independence, gave an added fillip to their lovemaking.

As the train sped past the glowering bulk of Durham Cathedral, Murdo reflected on the degree to which the bodies of women were his salvation. The virginal body of Miranda, too soon ruined by Jeremy's birth. The muscular sturdiness (so excitingly androgynous) of Kirstie, and her balance and strength which he loved to see her test; alas, the last time, too far.

He was sorry for women's suffering, the fact that they must endure monthly cramps and mess; and he, their irritable temper at such times. He sympathized with the agonies they underwent in childbirth. And afterwards, if like Miranda, they had been badly ripped.

He was bemused, as he reflected again on Suzanne's lying to him about not being able to have children. The silly girl did not realize that she always gave herself away in a falsehood. A slight tic appeared at the outer rim of her left eyelid. Ah well... she must, he supposed, have the illusion of control.

The train sped up, now it was well past Durham, nosing its way through the spreading darkness. He was impatient to be in London. The boy was a favourite student and he had indeed sounded desperate. Murdo had never forgotten that other one, a decade ago, a brilliantly promising mathematician who had noted his equations on lengths of rolled paper and then tacked them to the walls of his flat. And one day, having failed repeatedly to come up with the desired solution, he had taken down these reams and reams of paper, wrapped them about his body and set himself alight.

As the boy's family were in Peru, it was Murdo the police had called to identify the body. What he would never forget was how the inked fragments of the equations had burned themselves into the skin.

8

The Journal

It was years since menstruation had hit Suzanne this severely – like having been kicked in the midriff by a particularly vicious horse. She would have willingly given a tooth for one of Ada's tisanes for cramps. Shepherd's Purse was one ingredient she remembered, and Lady's Mantle.

In the master bathroom, she rummaged in the scarred oak cabinet above the marble sink. Its double doors, each with a classic keyhole but no key, were a palimpsest of deeply scored initials and cryptic messages. Today, the carved letters swam together. Through her dizziness, she sought to disentangle them. There were many *Callums*, heavily scored, and oddly placed, whether upside-down, longitudinal, or with the *allum* tucked inside the bulbous *C*. What a handful he must have been, she thought, grimacing at the idea of generic rambunctious boy. The initials *P. H.* also predominated. She assumed these identified some old school friend or young love of Callum's.

In the cabinet's jumble of old pill bottles, flattened tubes of shaving cream, and rock-hard bath salts (she must clear this lot out later), she seized on a box of Paracetamol and greedily gulped down two tablets with tap water. She sat on the old-fashioned toilet, whose frigid wooden seat set off a fresh set of contractions. She disliked this toilet, set up on a square tiled pedestal, against which she invariably stumbled when she got up during the night, eyes gluey with sleep. She detested its permanently discoloured bowl, the brown of nicotine-stained fingers, and its length of clanking chain looped from the ceiling like an empty manacle awaiting a prisoner.

She wondered why Murdo had never had a modern bathroom installed. There was a toilet (Murdo always said "lavatory") and wash-basin in a tiny, windowless cupboard on the ground floor, and a similar arrangement on the third floor of the house. How cramped and awkward it must have been for Kirstie and Miranda, when they changed diapers and toilet trained the children. Immediately, she regretted this thought. For a taunting image arose of a young, glossily pregnant Miranda standing naked before a full-length mirror, her arms folded protectively over her perfectly round, high belly. The pearly skin was so finely stretched, it verged on transparency. There was another human figure in this unwanted vision – a watcher or voyeur who studied the naked woman from the back, as well as her reflected front view in the mirror. Suzanne fought, and failed, being pulled inside this watcher so that she stared out through its eyes. What she sensed was not the hot stink of prurience she had feared, but a cooly clinical detachment. These eyes she unwillingly looked out of had the unflinching rigour of an exacto knife slicing through crisp paper. Suzanne felt that the observer's eyes, and the mind behind them, desired nothing more than to snip Miranda out of the scene, so that she became a three-dimensional paper doll that could be dangled, rotated in the air, examined from every angle, measured. Measured?

Suzanne groaned, leant forward, and using her hands to brace herself against the toilet seat, got unsteadily to her feet.

She groped her way back to bed and curled on her side, a hot water bottle clutched to her midriff. She whispered the word into the depths of the pillow, wishing it buried; then winced at the mental image of the glistening cruel points of a geometric compass.

She knew she must banish these thoughts. They were demons (doubt was a demon, as was jealousy) playing on her pain and vulnerability. You are inviting them in, she could hear Ada say. As a child she had pictured the demons with crab-like fingers, scrabbling through some chink in her mind. How to get rid of them? *Visualize, Suzanne. Visualize.*

She concentrated, then pictured herself walking through a spiralling mist at the base of the Eildon Hills. Where she stopped, she found a hollow dense with moss, as warm and dry as cat's fur. Here she lay down, feeling her pulse slow, and succumbed to a deep sleep, a drift downward into the innocent scent of the earth.

She passed a dreamless night. Then, toward dawn, woke with a start. There was a malicious-faced black cat sitting on the end of the bed. The animal's magnetic glare drew her, threatened to crush her very essence in the vise of its narrow skull. She shook herself properly awake, and became uncomfortably aware of the clammy rubber bag against her bare thigh and a dull ache in her pelvis. There was of course no actual cat. Not even a lingering hair. There were no pets of any kind in the house, which Suzanne thought a pity. Only the pair of peacocks that wandered the grounds outside, aloof and apparently secretive, until a flash of the male's ludicrously overwrought tail announced its presence. Or they loosed one of their shrill cries, which always made her think of a cat being tortured.

Her nightmare cat, she realized, was probably spawned by her reading about Marie Lamont, a young Scotswoman tried for witchcraft in 1662. Marie confessed that she and two other women came to the house of Allan Orr "in the likeness of kats, and followed his wyf into the chamber, where they took a herring out of a barrel and having taken a byte

off it, they left it behind them… his wyf did eat, and one
yaire after taking heavy disease, died."

Did Marie make her confession under the strictures of the
witch's bridle, Suzanne wondered, putting her hand tentatively to her own face as she ran the water for a bath. The bridle
had prongs that bit into the accused's cheeks. So that in her
delirium, Marie might well have believed herself to be a cat,
and the metal spikes digging into the flesh of her face, her
whiskers. Or was Marie subjected to the water trial, stripped
naked, her knees roped to her chest, before she was tossed into
the loch? If the accused sank, she was innocent and such innocent women often drowned. If she floated, she was deemed to
be a witch and then sentenced to be burned. Either way, the
water trial effectively reduced the female population.

Bringing her knees to her chest, half-floating in the
ancient clawed tub, Suzanne realized the full extent of these
women's humiliation. Bound in this way, their genitalia
would be completely exposed, as much as on any gynaecol-
ogist's table. The outer and the inner lips, the red gash of the
vaginal opening, cruelly on display to the judges and sundry
onlookers, curious or sadistic.

The "witch craze," some historians persisted in calling it.
An oddly deficient phrase, she thought, for a phenomenon
that had lasted nearly three hundred years and resulted in the
deaths of several million women. The misogyny that had
fuelled this phenomenon took on a particularly vile form in
the *Malleus Malificarum*, the papal document that had codified
procedures in the witchcraft trials. "Woman is a wheedling
and secret enemy. When a woman thinks alone, she thinks
evil… they are feebler both in mind and body." And this fee-
bleness meant that women were far more open to the devil's
blandishments. Woman would willingly lay her smooth hand
in the devil's horny one; then rut with goats; murder babies
and drink their blood; set a plague of warts upon a neigh-
bour.

"Woman is a wheedling and secret enemy." Suzanne feared that billions of men the world over still believed this unquestioningly, with terrible consequences for the women over whom they exerted their power. She often experienced her rage at misogyny as a physical illness, a soreness of body and spirit that she understood also as an unanswerable shame at being human. At these times, she readily identified with the radical lesbians of her acquaintance, who spoke and dealt solely with other women.

Suzanne's closest friend and London housemate, Gemma Tithe, was not quite that extreme. Gemma did have a few gay male friends and she was usually accepting of boys under the age of ten. But for the most part, Gemma viewed any male with cautious scepticism. In Gemma's opinion, the "new man" was pure invention. A lot of lip service but no fundamental change of heart. It was Gemma's reaction that had most hurt Suzanne when she told her friends of her impending marriage. Gemma, usually so forthright in her speech, had said not a word. To Suzanne's horror, Gemma had begun to cry, her brown eyes spilling repeatedly until a great damp patch spread across her lap, darkening the red of her skirt. When Suzanne tried to comfort her, Gemma pushed her away. What she said then hurt Suzanne more than her tears: "It is a terrible waste," she declaimed. "If you do this thing, it will end badly." The sound of her voice rendered the message even more ominous. Gemma spoke not in her customary fluting soprano, but in a coarse rasping, from a throat swollen with tears. So alien was this voice, Suzanne felt she was listening to an oracle. This was a prophetess who spoke from underground, half-choked on the sulphurous fumes that induced her trance.

She and Gemma had almost fought. "You don't know Murdo," Suzanne insisted angrily. "You have absolutely no basis for this judgement." Outside, sunlight suddenly hit the Thames, so that the walls of the room quivered in a pulsing light and shadow. We are in Plato's goddam cave, Suzanne thought, a flickering unreal place. As if to heighten this unreality, Gemma, who was so seldom still, sat rooted in her armchair, legs drawn up and crossed in front of her, like a compact black Buddha. Her uncharacteristic immobility and downcast eyes disturbed Suzanne as much as had the tears and ponderous prediction. She had left the house then and walked for hours. That night, she and Gemma slept, as they sometimes did, in the same bed.

"Shall I keep your room for you?" Gemma asked. "Yes," Suzanne said.

And so they had simply abandoned their mutual dilemma for the time being. Suzanne knew that Murdo and Gemma could never meet and be comfortable one with the other. For her sake, they would no doubt feign politeness. But she pictured them awkward as the wooden puppets she had drawn out of the wooden chest. Except that in Miranda's skilful hands, the puppets had doubtless moved fluidly, in an uncanny mimicry of life.

As she stood in Murdo's ancient kitchen and poured boiling water into the drip coffee pot, Suzanne recalled again the rasping note of Gemma's warning. She saw again the unfamiliar Murdo she had encountered in the outbuilding. The memory of his harsh words, the hard eyes, threatened to trigger a most terrible transformation: when love, with appalling swiftness, turns into dislike and even hate. Or if not hate, then an aching void where once love reigned. She had undergone such emotional reversals before, and the absoluteness of the inversion never ceased to amaze her. She was aware she tread dangerous ground, exacerbating what was probably a mere squabble by dwelling on Gemma's gloomy pronouncement.

It was true that she had risked much for Murdo's love, in order to co-habit with his vastness of spirit. She had lost friends. She had – superficially, at least – transgressed her own principles of uncompromised independence. She sipped at the thick black coffee and hoped it would fire her energy, for she felt heavy still, out of sorts. She was tempted simply to go on sitting at the bleached wooden table, to banish thought. Apart from the small upstairs study, this was the only room in the rambling house in which she felt entirely at ease. Here was an enduring domestic simplicity, clean, uncluttered surfaces, the gleaming, monumental Aga, a deep square sink of dark stone, the milky depths of the whitewashed walls and the cool silkiness of the flagstones beneath her feet. For almost four centuries, women had walked across these stones, on countless small journeys from oven to table, or sink to cupboard, or pacing back and forth, soothing a colicky child. Their labour, their constancy, had worked the stone as smooth as would an unending stream of water.

I thought Murdo was the Fire to my Water, she recalled; then grimaced that she had failed to banish thought. She got up, took a tub of Balkan yogurt from the refrigerator, and spooned it into a bowl. She ate, standing up, leaning against the sash of the kitchen's sole window. Murdo would not have approved. One ate at table, properly set, or not at all. In the past month, he had revealed himself to be irritatingly, rather than endearingly, stuffy. She had planned a kind of loving assault on his extremely conservative views on how and when one took nourishment. Now, however, the idea of his stringent correctness annoyed her exceedingly. She did not think she had the energy to bring about a shift in his attitude. Indeed, in view of what had happened before his abrupt departure, Murdo's fixation on ritualized table manners no longer seemed of importance.

She threw up the window with such force that it stuck half way up the sash. The sky was dark and sullen. The gust of wind that entered the kitchen smelt of rain. Suzanne sensed the urgency of an explosion to come. The air was uncomfortably electric. She heard the peacock's high-pitched scream, that disturbing cross between a cat's and a baby's cry. The cotton curtains at the window belled out, then whipped across her face. Suzanne stood on a chair, pushing down on the raised window with all her strength. It would not budge.

She must get the window closed. Her anxiety was not so much about the damage the rain might do to the plaster walls. What obsessed her was the notion that the unsettled weather, that force trying to push its way into the house, was somehow associated with her burgeoning doubts about Murdo. *Weather made the first gods.* Outside, it seemed, her old Watchtowers were in rebellion against her. Earth, Water, Fire, and Air were stirring, shaking, brewing up turmoil. She must keep this force outside for now. At least until she could garner all her resources.

She went looking for a hammer. A few firm, gentle taps, judiciously aimed, and she was sure she could get the window to close.

She found no tools of any kind in the kitchen drawers or cupboard, nor in the musty closet under the main staircase. She knew there was no point searching in Murdo's study, so she ventured for the first time since Murdo had shown her the house, up to the third floor. In fact, he had taken her into only one room on that floor – a room with an excellent view of the Eildon Hills, and otherwise empty, but for a single chair. There were four other doors on the third floor, all of them closed, and all leading to rooms in various states of disrepair. So Murdo had told her that first day. Once, these had been the children's rooms, he said. A bedroom each, a playroom and a room for the nanny.

In the first two rooms she entered, Suzanne found absolutely nothing except peeling wallpaper and scattered mouse droppings. In the third, there was again a single wooden chair (identical to the first) and tacked to the wall, a poster advertising a Pink Floyd concert. Also, on the floor of the cupboard, a white enamel chamber pot with a red handle. All this time, Suzanne was edgily aware of the thickening gloom outside and the wind rattling slates on the roof. This wind, with its dense odour of looming rain, seemed occasionally to touch her, even though all the windows on this floor were tightly closed. These gusts, which brushed her face and stirred her long skirt about her ankles, acted like a goad. She was becoming increasingly frantic. Reason told her that there was absolutely no need for this urgent search. She could, after all, simply mop up any water that came in the window. The flagstone floor would be basically impervious, and her original fear about damage to the plaster walls was probably unfounded. As yet another gust of wind belled out her skirt, she began to wonder whether her unconscious had manufactured this task; whether the need for a hammer was just a pretext to search the house in its entirety. And yet why would she feel the need for justification to go through rooms that were a part of Murdo's home? Wasn't simple curiosity or restlessness sufficient reason?

Even as she posed these questions to herself, the air about her crackled, as if the gathering point of the storm were here under the slate roof. The back of her neck prickled. She felt she tottered at the edge of a horrendous combustion, and that she must get out quickly. This force, she realized, was a variation on what she had experienced yesterday at the base of the staircase. Once again, she felt she was trespassing, transgressing or interfering in a world not properly her own. But she was alert as well to the possibility that this force was of her own making; that she was projecting some essential discomfort or guilt about her situation with Murdo. Whatever its origin, she knew she must face and go through it.

She pushed on to the last room. Above her, thunder boomed just as she grasped the brass knob. She opened the door, and was surprised to see not bare floor, but a stretch of blue carpet, patterned with darker blue flowers. Against the wall opposite the door stood a wooden chest of drawers, decorated with bright stencilled designs. The paint looked as if it had been applied by a child, with a determined but unsteady hand. Suzanne found this earnest imperfection charming. She stood a moment, utterly beguiled by the clumsy red hearts, the meandering dots of purple and green, which at a distance made a sprig of lilac, and a pair of slim white arcs, barely joined, which nevertheless caught the purity of winged flight.

This simple form moved her in some profound way she did not fully comprehend. Suzanne stood looking at the piece of furniture that was so obviously a relic of a young girl's passage into puberty. What she experienced was a palpable sense of loss, as deeply visceral as the ache she felt on waking after dreams in which Ada was still alive.

The source of this loss eluded her, although she guessed that this hand-painted chest had probably belonged to Miranda, and that it was Miranda whose wavering hand had applied the paint, in all the heady hope of youth, when everything is yet to come and one's immortality seems assured.

But death had come to Miranda far earlier than to most women of her generation and class. Had she lived, Miranda would now be in her fifties, Suzanne calculated. Yet she could not project the virginal girl of the photograph forward through time. That face resisted her efforts to picture it lined or haggard. Miranda was the rose petal preserved in amber.

She is my predecessor, Suzanne told herself, and, determined to see what lay inside the drawers, she entered the room. Her curiosity made a sharp taste in her mouth. Like blood when you bite your tongue, she thought. And I ought to do just that. Bite back the desire to pry and search out details of these two women who were once joined to Murdo. I am like Bluebeard's wife, snooping in closed rooms when he is absent. But, of course, I have no expectations of finding cadavers hanging from chains, no shrunken severed heads nestled in gauze.

She hesitated before opening the top drawer of the chest, and glanced at the window, where her eye was filled by a yellow-white spear of lightning. Still the rain did not come. There was only that tense electric space of yearning. The restless weather seemed to have taken her over, as she had sometimes seen weather take Ada over. Rolling naked in rumpled sheets to the rhythm of a storm. Dancing about the room in movements mimicking the wild surge of wind wrapping the house. For Ada, this was no self-indulgence, but a quest for consonance with the elements.

Suzanne believed she now moved at one with the turbulence beyond the window; that her own curiosity was pricked into action by the very explosive power of the air. She pulled the drawer open, and just as she lifted out the single object lying there, the rains loosed. They fell like a densely meshed curtain of lead, reinforcing Suzanne's sense of foreboding, of being swept into a drama against her conscious will. The desire to know something of her predecessors was paramount. She could not leave the two women as they had been, faceless and without substance. They had entered Murdo's soul. They were an inescapable part of the life she lived with him, and of his being. She walked in their footsteps.

Of course, it would be simpler and tidier simply to ignore them. Yet the very walls demanded that she know them. The smell of family life that had invaded her the previous day was only the beginning. If she failed to seek some knowledge of Miranda and Kirstie, Suzanne feared the house would expel her. And consequently, banish her from that spiritual union she so desired to cultivate with Murdo.

One ignores the demands of the dead at one's peril. One of her mother's essential precepts. Only a few clues, she told herself, and she could imagine the rest. Construct a remembrance of Miranda and Kirstie, where in fact she had none.

In the top drawer of the chest lay a small journal. She opened it, briefly surveyed the large, looping script and then shut the covers quickly again. How sacrosanct is a journal when its author is dead? Suzanne's instinct was to take the little book down to the kitchen, with all its absorbent, comforting surfaces. Miranda would often have sat at the kitchen table, her feet pressed into the known hollows of the stone floor, her hand steady as she spooned homemade vegetable purée into the baby's mouth. The baby whose picture Suzanne had held.

It was only then it dawned on Suzanne that there were no pictures of Murdo's children in the house. Or at least, in none of the rooms she and Murdo had used during the past three weeks. Was this deliberate on his part, a symbolic gesture that only he and she mattered? Or was the absence of the children's images evidence of his estrangement from his family? His remarks about Jeremy had been anything but loving.

In the kitchen Suzanne put the cloth-covered journal on the table, and did a perfunctory mop up of the water that had come in the window. The rain had stopped. The air smelled new-washed. Trying the window sash again, she found that it now slid easily up and down.

She sat at the table and studied Miranda's signature in the flyleaf of the journal. Her handwriting was a shock, as round and characterless as a very young girl's first attempt at signing her name. The *a*'s were apples; the capitals *N* and *M* were toppling mountains. The signature's sole assertion was the oblique dash underlining the surname, as though to emphasize, or to remind herself, that she was indeed Miranda Napier.

What entries there were, were sparse, all written in the same childlike hand. Flicking through, Suzanne saw that the

journal covered only a few months of 1960 and that most of
the pages were empty. She was puzzled by three columns of
numbers that appeared on the journal's final page, headed by
the letters *Br*, *W* and *Bo*. As she read, the significance of these
columns gradually dawned on her, and she was beset with a
disgust and a pity that brought her close to tears.

May 6, 1960. Murdo says I may see baby Jeremy tomorrow,
but for 15 minutes only. He will tire me, Murdo says. Nanny
Oliphant has found a wet nurse for Baby. I must be reassured.
This is for the best, they tell me. Already, my milk is going.

May 15, 1960. We have begun the daily measurements.
Murdo has bought a new cloth tape measure, pale green and
the numbers all glittering gold, like the sparkle on Christmas
wrapping paper. I will soon be back to my old self, Murdo
says. What a pouter pigeon I have become, he says. I cried
with the wanting to see Baby Jeremy, while Murdo was off
with his telescope.

May 27, 1960. My breasts are quite without milk now.
While Murdo was in Edinburgh, Nanny Oliphant let me in
to see baby. The wet nurse was feeding him. She is a kind,
rosy woman. But the sight of Baby Jeremy sucking at her
nipple hurt me terribly. A gnawing deep inside. Is this jealousy? He is my baby. He does not tire me.

June 5, 1960. It is true that the pills stop the gnawing sensation. My sleep is thick and woolly. Sometimes just to lift a
teaspoon seems a very heavy thing indeed. Baby Jeremy is
well. When I saw him in the morning, he smiled, looking like
one of the little angels in the convent chapel.

Nanny Oliphant is very strict about my time with him.
I believe she and Murdo have had words.

June 7, 1960. I do not like at all when the measurements
are done with me in front of the mirror. I do not like to see

the truth of what Murdo says, although he tries to be gentle
and strokes my hair. I know my breasts droop a little now, and
my tummy is not as flat as it was. There are little silver lines
that run along the surface of my thighs and on my bottom.
Murdo pointed them out to me. We must mark down the
measurements each day, he says, so that I can see and be
cheered by my own progress. He is working out a special
exercise program and diet for me. I want my sweet girl back
just as she was, he says.

June 15, 1960. I dream of running away with Baby
Jeremy.

June 17, 1960. So weary. Nanny would not let me hold
baby today. My arms limp like dangling sausages. Like my
poor puppets without me to animate them. Cannot animate
myself.

June 25, 1960. New pills. When I try to walk, my feet feel
as if they are stuck in oozing mud. I want very much to hold
baby, but cannot walk to the nursery.

June 27, 1960. I sleep too much now, but cannot seem to
stop myself. I do not dream.

June 30, 1960. Still, I do not dream. Murdo feeds me
with a spoon. Is this the nursery?

July 3, 1960. Who is Baby Jeremy? Did I dream him
when I could still dream?

There was no more. The remainder of the journal, with the
exception of the three columns on the back page, was stark-
ly empty. An accusatory blankness, signifying what?
Enervation? Collapse? Had Miranda been hospitalized? Was
she still alive, locked in a bone-white room, crying for Baby
Jeremy?

Suzanne felt there was a wolf ripping at her entrails. The
menstrual cramps were back with a vengeance. She put her
head to her knees, dug her nails deep into her thighs. She was
sick. She was cold. She was afraid all she had read might be

the truth; that this man she had married, with whom she had the unfailingly hot and luscious sex, had been vilely cruel to a young and vulnerable woman. Here was abuse that came just too close to home. *Home.* She winced at the very word. This damp and gloomy mausoleum was not her home. She had thought Murdo's body her home. She found she was crying, whether for herself or the young Miranda, she did not know.

What had the woman in the shop said? "That Napier devil ruined that young girl's life." But that had been a much younger Murdo? Was it possible he had outgrown this twisted notion of love Miranda's journals described in such excruciating simplicity? Was Murdo's great suffering partly guilt for what his young self had done to Miranda?

Breasts, Waist, Buttocks. These were Miranda's measurements at the back of the journal. Could Murdo — her sensual, tragic, contemplative Murdo — have done these things? Perhaps the journal was a fake, produced by one of the children in adolescence, in a fit of pique. Or authored by Miranda, but delusional, the ramblings of a post-partum depression.

He ruined that young girl's life. Was that really what she heard? She could hardly go into the village and interrogate the women in the shop.

I must get away, she thought. Go down to London. Sit quietly in my old room. Talk to Gemma.

She opened a tin of consommé soup, dosing it liberally with ground black pepper to fight the cramps. Almost immediately she felt better and went upstairs to pack her bag. She decided to take the bus to Edinburgh where she would catch a train. Consulting the timetable, she found she still had a good three hours to spare, even given the mile walk to the bus stop.

Restless, she wandered the grounds, and found herself again in the overgrown apothecary's garden. From that

vantage point, all she could see of the house was the tower
with its triangular cap of slate. She was seized with an urgent
desire to see inside it, despite the tacit rule that this was
Murdo's private sanctuary.

The door at the base of the tower was unlocked. Inside
was a winding stair with steep steps of buff-coloured stone.
Suzanne started up. There was no banister. Only a thick rope,
looped through metal rings set in the thick wall. This she
gripped tightly all the way up.

She emerged suddenly into a well of dusky light. Just
above her, she saw where the steps ended, culminating in a
solid stone platform. She pulled herself up the remaining
steps by the final length of rope, and stood blinking in the
thin white light that penetrated the tower's cruciform windows that were more slits than crosses.

She was a little breathless. This she attributed to the fact
that the windows let in so little air. Just below one of the
windows sat Murdo's telescope. A dull black insect with a
particularly long proboscis. She was surprised at how small
the instrument was. Each evening, when Murdo withdrew
for several hours to the tower, she had pictured him with a
machine at least as large as himself, complete with a complexity of knobs and dials. She had imagined too, a substantial desk littered with papers, each bearing those rivers of
runic script that were his craft and art.

Instead, there was a small, plain table, absolutely bare,
with the exception of an oil lamp identical to the one
Suzanne had used in the outbuilding. The table had a single
drawer. She hesitated, then pulled it open. She was fully
aware of the irony of her probing – she who had so rejoiced
at their mutual sustaining separateness.

Inside the drawer lay an olive green portfolio. She drew
it out carefully and laid it on the table. The portfolio contained a sheaf of oilskin paper, which Suzanne at first took to
be untouched. But on closer inspection, she saw that each

sheet did in fact bear a faint mark. In all cases, this was a curve, made with a pen so fine-tipped, so unwaveringly applied, as to be almost invisible to the naked eye. Each of the sheets was numbered in sequence.

Inside the back leaf of the portfolio, tucked in a flap, was a list of dates corresponding to each of the numbered oilskin pages. This page was titled "Kirstie." The writing was Murdo's. She could make no sense of either the drawn curves or the list of dates. Here at least she had uncovered no damning evidence.

She tucked the oilskin sheets neatly back into the portfolio and replaced it in the drawer. On impulse, she decided to take a look through the telescope. She was perturbed when she put her eye to the aperture and saw only blackness. She tilted the glass upward and stepped back to check its position. It was aimed truly at the light entering the window. She looked through again and there was only blackness. A cap, she thought. No doubt there was a cap to protect the glass from dust. But when she examined the end of the telescope, she found nothing of the kind. She put the tip of her finger gingerly against the end glass. It was rough, almost grainy, to the touch. Peering closer, Suzanne saw that the lens of the telescope had been painted a flat black.

She ran down the winding staircase, perplexed and a little sickened at Murdo's duplicity. All those hours he had spent in his tower, supposedly studying the stars, he had in fact seen nothing.

In the house she grabbed her overnight bag. She paused only to make sure she had plenty of tampons for the train journey down to London. She did not leave Murdo a note.

9

By the Thames

"Sugar?" Gemma got the word out despite the fact it caused her pain. She could pronounce it only with the greatest difficulty. Even in its apparently less refined forms (brown, demerara) she detested the substance, would not by choice, have it in her house. Honey, yes. Honey was guiltless, whether dusky or translucent. Bees made honey, manufactured it out of their busy communal life, and the workers' obeisance to their queen was purely instinctual, a demand written into their cells. The humans who collected the honey were not bound to do so, but went about their business cheerfully and lovingly, or so Gemma imagined. Beekeepers moved through that droning and humming and swarming as if through some benign atmosphere. They were patient, vigilant people and the honey derived from their labour shone innocently, like their eyes.

This was not pure fantasy. Gemma had indeed met several beekeepers, all of whom were gentle taciturn people, with a childlike gaze. So for Gemma, honey sang, where *sugar* screamed. She could not abstract sugar from its historical burden. She could not look at it packaged in snowy white bags or pristine sealed boxes, without an accompanying vision of black and brown backs split open under the whip, or flesh gouged by chains. She could not even think the word *sugar* without picturing skin seared by the master's brand, or workers' backs roasted as they hung on a spit over a fire, the punishment reserved for runaways.

For those people who protested that the horrors of the sugar plantations were over centuries ago ("It's all beet sugar now – European, you know."), Gemma reserved a particularly nasal braying laugh, absolutely purged of mirth. Did they really believe the evils of the past disappeared just because they wished it so? Were they so naive? Or was it a question of moral convenience?

Now Suzanne too. Had she really not considered where Murdo's ancestors got their money? Had she not put the inheritance of a mouldering Scottish mansion together with Murdo's childhood in the Caribbean? Where there was no doubt another house, also mouldering, also sprawling, with a wide veranda facing a glittering sea and another facing the fields, the stage from which the master commanded his army of black, brown, and mulatto bodies. His property. On whose toil he built his small empire.

"Sugar?" she asked Suzanne again. She spat the word out, and having to repeat it, grew even more tense.

Suzanne did not answer. She seemed lost in some meandering thought. She stared at the window, although there was nothing to see but dull night sky and the haze of her own reflection.

Gemma reached for the bottle of single malt she had set in the middle of the floor. She and Suzanne sat, as they so often had in the past, cross-legged on the carpet, a ring of Gemma's scatter cushions ranged round them. Just as in days past, Gemma had dimmed the lights and lit a tall white candle, set in a wrought iron holder on the floor beside the bottle.

This candle had a triple function. The first was aesthetic. Gemma loved to watch the lambent flame play upon the amber in the bottle. The second was emotional, for Gemma preferred a soft illumination, especially when talking with friends. She associated harsh light with the institutions in which she so often did battle: council offices, police offices, courts, clinics, social service cubicles. The candle's third function was admonitory. If Gemma reached for the bottle and the candle wobbled, she knew it was time to stop drinking.

Gemma had a healthy fear of drunkenness; not so much because of her father, but because getting drunk (in the privacy of her own home) was often so terribly enticing. There were nights when she craved senselessness, to get so benumbed she would not have felt a needle thrust into her thumb. Because she simply could no longer bear thinking of the stinking world she lived in, and of what men did, and of what they made women do.

From the look of Suzanne, Gemma wondered if it might be a night for simply snuffing out the candle, and drinking herself stupid. Never had she seen her friend in such a state. Suzanne's usually erect shoulders slumped forward, as though at any moment she might collapse into a self-protective huddle. Her hair, too, fell forward over her face. She was hiding, thought Gemma, a thoroughly uncharacteristic attitude for Suzanne.

"Suzanne!" Gemma clapped her hands together so hard that her palms stung. Time to break through this torpor, an insidious state that Gemma always feared as infectious. Not a state for any woman to be in, and to see Suzanne succumb was nauseating. Gemma realized she was terribly disappointed. She had wanted Suzanne to come back from that wretched Murdo male, with her eyes blazing in indignation, furious at her own grievous error in marrying. For after all, what other result could there be at the end of the day? Marriage was dangerous to women's health. Gemma still could not grasp why Suzanne imagined she might be the exception.

"What? Sorry, Gemma. What were you saying about sugar?"

Gemma heaved one of her histrionic sighs, and poured herself a hefty shot of scotch. "Suzanne Clelland," she ordered, in a perfect mimicry of her old school headmistress, lips pursed just so and eyebrows raised in pantomime fury, "If you do not immediately reveal why you have returned so abruptly from your bower of bliss, I will set you the task of plucking ten somewhat past-their-best chickens."

Suzanne laughed, which brought about an instantaneous transformation, much to Gemma's relief.

"Oh, Gemma. I feel I've been away so long."

You have been, Gemma wanted to say. You've been away too long in some godawful illusory world, shackled to some man unworthy to rinse out your underwear. But it was not yet the moment for provocation, she reasoned. So instead, she handed Suzanne a drink.

"Can you talk?" Gemma asked.

"Hmm." Again, the hesitation was unlike Suzanne.

"Verbal abuse?" Gemma put the question as tentatively as she could.

"No… more simple confusion."

"About what?"

"About my predecessors. About the two women he was married to before me."

So Gemma heard about Suzanne's discovery of the marionettes in the outbuilding, of Murdo's outburst and abrupt departure, and of the contents of Miranda's post-partum journal.

"You need to talk to his children," Gemma said, when Suzanne had told her everything. "I mean, if you really must go back, if you must carry this through…"

"To its end?"

"Well, yes. If you will." Gemma put on her posh voice in a somewhat vain attempt to distance herself from her own annoyance. When really, she wanted to shake Suzanne by her broad, elegant shoulders, and say: Leave him, just leave him. Put this foolishness behind you before he succeeds in sucking the life out of you.

They drank whisky until the dusky confines of the room dissolved. It seemed that the house was itself a floating world, drifting above the Thames. Time contracted. Gemma and Suzanne found themselves sitting so close together, their foreheads were touching. This was a ritual they had stumbled on some years ago, the elements being plentiful whisky, their penchant for honesty, darkness, and the river. What often came about was an evaporation of barriers between conscious and unconscious, between their separate selves. A kind of scrying through thought and non-thought that could miraculously yield insights fresh and clear. When they woke in the morning, they had sometimes lost the fullness of these revelations (and gained a sick headache), but a shimmering edge would remain, like the bright rim of a crystal glass. So that later in the day, they might be able to retrieve the idea in its wholeness.

They snuffed the candle out, talked on in the pungent darkness.

In the morning, this is what Suzanne remembered: Gemma saying that great sex did not necessarily lead to gnosis; that this was Suzanne's grand delusion. Gemma reading her a poem about a man obsessed with his own suffering, *I am the Widower, the unconsoled, the Prince of Aquitaine in his black tower.* And something more about the Black Sun of the Melancholia. Which was so terribly descriptive of Murdo that to hear these words read aloud had seemed like a personal invasion. You have been seduced by the Hanged Man, Gemma said. By his gloom and solipsism and inverted state in the world. The man who wrote the poem was mad, Gemma told her. He used to walk a lobster on a leash through the streets of Paris, and consorted with prostitutes. Ultimately, he hung himself.

Likely it was the prostitutes who helped him survive as long as he had, Suzanne thought. Well, yes, she had seen the Black Sun in Murdo's face. Was it a ploy, his manifest suffering a snare to hold her fast? A ploy that he might not consciously recognize as such, but still and all, a ploy. Certainly, she could not know for sure until she returned to Scotland and succeeded in getting him talking. And undid the silence that had so drawn her to him?

This is what Gemma recalled in the morning: Suzanne's description of a portrait of a dark Madonna, hung in a curtained alcove. Shadows outline her face, seep from her neck to her breast, gather in the palm of her outstretched hand. In her other arm she holds the naked baby, his tiny genitalia only just visible behind the foot he has pulled up in front of his body. As if vainly trying to shield himself from what is to come, his inevitable fate that the artist has made manifest in the child's flesh. For like his mother (who will also suffer), the agony of what is to come is prefigured in the gloom that has penetrated his plump thighs and calves and belly; even his chubby face is dominated by the dark that is his future. The child's eyes are fixed on the object he grasps in his two chubby hands. Not a toy, but a yarn winder, which looks exactly like an inverted cross. So that even at the age of one and a half, he is fully aware of the end to which he is progressing. The mother gazes adoringly at the boy on her knee. Gemma knows and detests this look, and avoids going to Italy for just that reason. Hundreds of mothers, on trains, in restaurants, on benches, in parks and in museums, gaze down adoringly at the infants in their arms. It is a look they reserve for their male children. Which explains, Gemma believes, a great deal about the nastily swollen ego of the Italian male.

All men, Gemma is convinced, revel in the idea of the slain god, the self-sacrificing saviour. Some, like Murdo, get fixated on the idea of themselves as suffering. Their agony becomes their art form, their justification for being.

After all Suzanne had told her, Gemma feared even more for her friend. The dark-browed Madonna and her child might well have something to do with the turbulent spirits whose presence Suzanne had sensed in the house. Or the spirits might be spawned by some old evil in the Caribbean, the preying restlessness of inherited guilt. Then again, the root of the disturbance might indeed have something to do with the way in which Murdo's first two wives lived. Or died.

Marriage was so dangerous to the health that it brought many women close to death. Gemma saw proof of this every day.

She did not plead with Suzanne not to return to Scotland. What had been done must be undone. Suzanne had to learn the truth, or as close as she could come to it.

The night before Suzanne left, they slept together in Gemma's bed, lying within the sphere of each other's body heat, occasionally touching each other, fleetingly and with affection. But without sex. Early on in their relationship, they recognized that if they were lovers, their friendship would be imperilled and likely end acrimoniously. So this was the sacrifice they made, in order to continue knowing each other. When they slept together, they would often dream fragments of each other's life, particularly in times of emotional turmoil.

So it was with considerable chagrin that Gemma repeated to Suzanne in the morning the three words that had pushed their way repeatedly into her dreams. Words she knew instinctively were meant for Suzanne.

"Alone, soiled, and ghosted," Gemma told her.

"Nice assonance," Suzanne replied. Gemma understood from this attempt at flipness, just how tense Suzanne was at the idea of returning to Scotland.

"Ghosted," Suzanne murmured, revealing her true state of grave apprehension.

"Talk to the children," Gemma said.

Then they hugged each other, two women with the same three words replaying in their heads.

10

A Frugal Meal

On the train back to Edinburgh, Suzanne leafed through her latest source book on witches – an illustrated treatise on familiars, with portraits of toads in little silk suits which made her laugh. She was grateful for the distraction; anything to take her mind off the looming reunion with Murdo.

She wanted very much to go back to him naked in a sense, staying true to the momentum of her initial risk in marrying him. Just as he might follow through the urgent energy of an equation as it wrote itself out in time.

Yet she could not escape the fact that Gemma's admonitions had fuelled the uncertainty as to who and what Murdo was.

Gemma was of course the most formidable of opponents when it came to the possible saving graces of the male. There were none, absolutely none, said Gemma. Suzanne knew, however, that her friend did allow the odd exception. But her toleration extended only to those very few gay men, all of whom had been subjected to – and passed – Gemma's rigorous tests. The slightest hint of condescension, or misogynist innuendo, and the male with the apparent saving grace was immediately struck from Gemma's good books.

With men, Gemma was quite merciless. And Suzanne fully understood her reasons. In Gemma's world, women were both centre and circumference and everything in between. They were her friends, her lovers, her raison d'être, her salvation. With women, Gemma was all things she could not bring herself to be with men: forgiving, consoling, supportive. Those she found hardest to forgive were the women who returned to live with their abusers. But even here, she would wrench her perspective round to some point of compassion. It is a hard thing, said Gemma, to throw off a yoke that has been thousands of years in the making. A yoke that women were so conditioned to wearing that they simply thought of it as the norm. "But the poor sod would perish without me." How often, Gemma would ask with tears in her eyes, had she heard that self-deluding rationalization?

Gemma's greatest successes were the abused women who did suddenly see the yoke for what it was. And threw it off. The most glorious of epiphanies, Gemma called this enlightenment; the dropping of the scales from eyes still ringed with bruises.

For those women who did not see, who returned to the men who had promised to change, Gemma did literally pray. If she learned that one of these women had been maimed or murdered by the man who had sworn to transform, she came close to despair. Then quite deliberately, she gave full vent to her rage, donning the boxing gloves she had bought for exactly this purpose, and battering away at a punching bag strung up in a small, otherwise empty, top-floor room. Yes, she had painted the outline of a phallus on the punching bag, as well as a coiled mass that represented matted chest hair. And yes, she would eventually collapse in a corner, sweaty, untidy, and tear-stained. But largely emptied of the rage. At least, until the next time.

There must be more than just a *few* exceptions, Suzanne argued with herself. Murdo must be an exception. The idea of his multi-chambered silence, his heat and force in bed, pulled at her still. Or was she indeed deluded? Was she projecting her own desires on to a man who was not only manipulative but tainted?

She found she could not concentrate at all on her book. She was in a most uncomfortable state of suspension, moving toward a result she could in no way predict. Like the randomness, she supposed, of Murdo's wilful electrons. She wondered ruefully if she might somehow be moving backward. If by marrying Murdo, she were simply satisfying some atavistic urge to come under the thrall of the male. He who brings home the bleeding meat; who brandishes the flaming torch when the wolves creep close. Or was her desire for him rooted in something far more pernicious: her unconscious attraction to the doom that she sometimes perceived in his ingrained melancholy? What was the essence of her bond to Murdo?

"Beware the double. Learn to distinguish the false image from the true." Another of Ada's gnomic utterances. As was: "The object of your desire will often ring hollow." Like a false chime, Ada elucidated, a sound that will set your teeth on edge, and then the nerves. Well, one knew what followed.

As far as Suzanne was aware, Ada had always managed to avoid the bitter fruit of disappointed love. The Russian and Polish sailors who returned year after year were never in her life for more than three or four days at a time. If Ada missed one more than another when he left, she gave her daughter no indication. As Suzanne grew older, she came to understand that Ada's great love would always be her craft, and the elements from which it was born. Her mother took most delight in that invisible world where she consorted with daimons feathered, jewelled, and sleek. Those daimons could also be duplicitous, more so than human kind, said Ada. So she proceeded cautiously in the spirit realm – as in the real one – lest she be fooled.

Suzanne had been fooled, by men and women both. Her instincts, she knew, were not as finely developed as her mother's. Yet she had been fortunate. When betrayed or belittled, in friendship or in love, Suzanne had never crashed too badly. Nor had she become embittered, one of the worst results by her reckoning.

This most recent leap she had taken – this marriage – was in part a kicking against constraints. She had begun to feel more and more hedged in by the expectations put upon her as a "feminist" writer. The increasing pressure to align herself with a particular faction made her restless and angry. She sensed they wanted her to play the elegant Amazon, to swear off men just as people swore off alcohol and tobacco. "You could be a media star, a figurehead. Exploit the power structure for the sake of the movement." How often had she heard that? She had come to loathe the very idea of feminism as a "movement."

How did it happen? You started out with a wonderful essential insight, fresh as a mint-laden wind, and you ended up with a hydra-headed institution plagued by petty quarrels and divisions.

Suzanne was herself most passionate about clear vision. A seeing through and back to the female soul in its primitive shining state. Before parts of it were split off and debased. By men, yes. But more accurately by a patriarchal structure that manipulated and brainwashed men, inculcating a craven fear of women that so easily became hatred. Men took woman's virgin self and broke and defiled it and traded it and paid coin for it. And her sexual self they cheapened and called a dirty whore and paid coin for it. Her instinctual wisdom they called witch and burned.

The most terrible irony of all was that men were themselves suffering because of their depredations on women's souls. And for the most part, they simply did not see. And so the trail of blood and despoilment went on. And we are all cheated, men and women both, thought Suzanne. And would be as long as the heinous historic conditioning continued, and men the world over persisted in not seeing that they did not see.

Like Gemma, Suzanne did occasionally give way to despair. She fantasized sometimes about a total escape. In a daydream she would not have confessed even to Gemma, she was a round-eyed lemur, purely innocent, a miracle of agility, at one with blue sky and green leaf and sturdy branch. Eating, defecating, scratching, swinging faultlessly arm over arm through space. Looking, always looking, out of those startled orbs. Having – and this was the most blissful aspect – a very circumscribed consciousness. A cowardly fantasy, in other words. A fantasy of absolute retreat.

Whereas she was in reality in the thick of human embroilments. Not the least of which was the attempt to honour and show all proper respect to millions of women who had died the most terrible deaths, who had undergone assaults on body and soul that she could never imagine. And she had married, taken a course so diametrically opposed to the one expected of her that many of her former friends would forever brand her an outcast. Nor had she married a demonstrably "new" man, but a very visibly older one who did in certain aspects resemble the greying patriarch. Neither was there anything observably androgynous in Murdo's face. It was too rugged, too broad, too marked by time. Yet she loved Murdo's face, the gouges and vulnerability he wore with such utter dignity.

She was therefore shocked when she got off the train at Waverley Station, to see a man so like Murdo, he might be his twin. Yet although the features matched exactly, this man's face seemed somehow brutish, perhaps because his eyes were narrowed in nasty glare.

For an instant – no more – Suzanne stood frozen on the platform. The Murdo double glared at her, with a fixity that

left no doubt that she was its object. She had the wild
thought that this was a twin brother Murdo had never mentioned. But surely, she reasoned, such an omission would be
excessively secretive. For a twin was a defining thing. Twins
were bound forever, even if they never saw one another.
They had a singleness that was written into their cells, if not
into their souls.

She remembered a woman Ada had counselled whose
twin had died at birth. This woman was tortured by dreams
of the other baby being pulled away and sucked backward
down a black, windy tunnel. She heard her twin crying, she
said, and would wake from the dream with fear freezing her
throat and pity swelling her chest, to a point that she had to
fight for breath. She began to avoid sleep and was literally
rocking on her feet when she came to see Ada. Who pre-
scribed a potent sleeping draught, and induced an alternative
dream in which the woman was able to embrace her twin's
spirit and hold her fast in her own breast.

As Suzanne thought of Ada, Murdo's double came
toward her. She could see the redness of his neck and the
sweat on his brow; noted how inappropriately the man was
dressed for such a warm day in buttoned-up shirt and tie and
a suit jacket. Why did some men, she wondered, have such
difficulty in forsaking their uniforms?

When he spoke, harshly, so that his hot breath burned her
face, she put away all foolish thoughts of a twin. This was
Murdo, inescapably so. The Murdo to whom she had legally
bound herself. She supposed she had entertained that absurd
notion of a twin simply to distance herself from this frowning,
sweating man. She was actually repulsed by his expression, a
glower that he had directed at her across the platform, and still
kept on his broad, flushed face. He pushed his head so close to
hers that she had an urge to slap him. But, of course, desisted.

"Whatever possessed you," he hissed in her ear, "to travel
second-class and dressed like… like some street person?"

"Murdo, don't be ridiculous." She spoke quietly, making a supreme effort to control her own temper.

There was an unpleasant bloodlessness to his mouth that matched his clipped, heartless tone. Unsure of her next move, Suzanne bent to pick up her bag, and swung it over her shoulder. She began to walk away from him, quickly. She did not look back. Her stride was long and free. At that point, she felt she could walk forever, so long as Murdo was always receding behind her.

Such was her anger that only physical movement could keep it quelled. His remark about her "state" of dress struck her as totally ludicrous – she was wearing jeans and a perfectly respectable T-shirt. Nor did she wish to dwell too much on the irony that they had travelled from London on the same train, sealed off from one another in their separate compartments. She had never in her life travelled first-class even when she could afford it.

She heard Murdo call her name; then the steady thump of his feet, as he came running after her. She did not turn around. Then she felt a hand on her shoulder, settling lightly as a moth. She turned and looked in horror at the nakedness of his pain. He seemed to be on the edge of tears, and his evident vulnerability intensified all the marks of aging on his face, the complex fretwork around his eyes, and the shadows that gathered under them. In that instant, she understood how much closer he was to death than she. She experienced a great rush of compassion, undercut by guilt. She had not meant to make him weep.

"I am so sorry, my dear." His cheek was wet against hers. His voice had regained its normal timbre, low and strong, with its sensual resonant burr. "My nerves are a little frayed, I fear." He took a crumpled handkerchief from his pocket and wiped his eyes.

It was then that Suzanne recalled Murdo's student. Up to that point, she realized she had only half believed in this student in distress. The whole episode had suggested the convenient deliverance. But his evident distress seemed proof enough that he had recently undergone some ordeal.

"Your student?"

"Ah," he said. Murdo's *ahs* were always followed by a little trough of silence. Suzanne had grown accustomed to this habit, and stood waiting.

"A bit messy, I'm afraid. Aspiring mathematicians are frequently very proficient with an exacto knife." He lifted his right arm so that his shirt cuff fell back, exposing his wrist. With his left hand, he mimed a long, deep cut through the vein.

Suzanne shuddered. "Surely he didn't die?"

"No, no. Thank God. The downstairs neighbours heard him hit the floor, and came up to investigate. They had exchanged keys, fortunately, to care for each other's cats if one or the other went away. Most fortunate. Most fortunate, indeed."

"Will he be all right?"

"Ah… well, it depends, I suppose, on his recuperative powers, on his degree of commitment. On the whole, however, I suppose not. He should probably pursue some less demanding discipline. Or is it too late for that? It would appear he simply hasn't the stamina, a lack I should perhaps have perceived much earlier on."

"But you must not blame yourself."

"Oh no, by no means. It's that wh…"

He could not finish, but broke down again suddenly, burying his head in her shoulder. Then just as abruptly, this renewed show of emotion was over. Murdo knelt down and opened his suitcase; withdrew a clean, folded white handkerchief and dabbed at his face.

In silence, they walked together to the underground parking lot where Murdo had left the Bentley, and so they proceeded home, with barely a word said. Suzanne checked, as circumspectly as possible, Murdo's continuing high colour

and the somewhat alarming contrast of his pallid lips. Here
was the spectre of death again. Yet she understood that it was
as much the deaths of Miranda and Kirstie that haunted her,
as any rational fear for Murdo.

She must get him to speak of them, even if only a little.
For neither she nor they could be at peace until Murdo
opened the way. Her ignorance of the two women was an
affront to their spirits.

The difficulty was that she did not know quite how to
open the question. Neither she nor Murdo had yet alluded
to the scene he had made before his departure for London.
She did not want to mention Miranda's diary, not only
because its content was so unflattering to Murdo, but also
because she did not want him to know she had deliberately
searched the house.

Would he interpret her interest in Kirstie and Miranda as
an insensitive curiosity? Or worse, an ill-founded jealousy?
How was she to begin?

When the car stopped in front of the sprawling house
with its neatly capped turret, Suzanne had to control an
involuntary shudder. She recalled with some discomfort the
electric force that had repelled her and the odours that had
overwhelmed her at the foot of the stairs.

Once inside, they bathed – separately. It occurred to
Suzanne as she lay in the bath, that apart from Murdo's putting his head on her shoulder, they had not embraced. There
had been no kiss of any description, perfunctory, forgiving or
tentative. She presumed that when at last they were in bed
together again, they would fall naturally into the shapes
forged by their heat and desire. That would not be the place
to raise the question, she realized. Not between those close-
woven white sheets in a bed where he might well once have
lain with Miranda. And then with Kirstie. No, she would definitely not ask in bed, for all its boundless intimacy and wondrous shared breathing.

They prepared a frugal meal. Slices of cheese and whole grain bread, apples, pears and a dollop of yogurt. Murdo suggested that they set the table in the cavernous dining hall. In the month or so they had spent together in the house, they had always eaten in the kitchen.

The dining hall seemed to be designed for human beings of gargantuan stature, with its lofty ceiling and a floor that Suzanne thought might easily accommodate a hundred dancers. Yet who would choose to dance in a room so fundamentally inhospitable? She found its spartan aspect quite chilling. The furnishings consisted of the huge dining table set under the fan-shaped window, four wooden armchairs set about a gaping stone fireplace, an entire wall covered in a faded red velvet curtain (for what purpose she could not fathom, other than to keep out the oozing damp in the stone). The only other object in the room was a six-foot-wide mirror in a heavy carved wooden frame. The silver backing was so worn that the mirror had little, if any, reflecting power. Once, she had stood tiptoe to stare into its depths, and had encountered only the vaguest form, slightly twisted, much like the image that would be thrown back by a stagnant pond.

She wondered if the room had ever been warmed by the laughter of children, or of women easy in each other's company. Ada would know. Ada would have been able to hear the voices that had once echoed off the stone walls. For Suzanne, this dour room was a place she could imagine punishment being meted out, or discipline rendered. A most unkind place.

Tomorrow she would resist if Murdo again suggested they eat in this unpleasant room. Today, she would make allowances for his anxiety over his student's brush with death. Today Murdo must be catered to.

She was relieved to see he had regained his normal colour, his full lips firm and flushed with pink. He spread the merest dab of butter on a slice of bread. He ate carefully, without dropping a crumb.

Suddenly, there was a high-pitched scream, the sound of a creature terribly tortured. Suzanne dropped the spoon with which she had been ladling yogurt into a glass bowl. Simultaneously, the room went dim. A dark shape smothered the light from the fan-shaped window above them.

Suzanne looked up and saw the peacock, its wings spread full, displaying all its absurd male beauty, the jewel-like eyes glittering and unseeing. The bird turned its head round to stare in at her. These real eyes were beady, malevolent.

She was surprised to hear Murdo laugh. "Ah," he said, "did the big, bad peacock frighten you?"

She was shocked by his stupidly superior tone. She had not thought him capable of that kind of automatic condescension. And because she was annoyed and disappointed with him, she decided not to wait. She would broach her question now. Leap now, as he had leapt, mocking her as unthinkingly as a callow boy.

"Is keeping the peacocks a family tradition, Murdo? Or was it Kirstie or Miranda who brought them here?"

"Kirst –." Murdo spat out a piece of bread; then secreted it inside his napkin. He pulled back his chair from the table. He sat rigidly erect, a pharaoh on his throne.

"Please," he began, the word more order than request. "Do not let me hear you speak their names. They are dead, gone. We live now. You and I. They can no longer matter. That is the way with the dead."

He reached out as though to touch her arm; then apparently reconsidered. He sat back again, resuming the silent regal pose.

Suzanne was perplexed, and still a little stunned by his sweeping dismissal of his first two wives. And what of memories, she was about to ask him. What of the persistence of their images in your mind? But in this mood, she speculated, he might well simply quibble; perhaps ask: "But what is mind, my dear Suzanne? Are you certain that mind exists?"

As she wondered, Murdo gestured to the peacock, which still displayed himself in full.

"They are a family tradition, yes. My great-great-grandfather purchased a pair for reasons I cannot fathom. One learns to ignore them after a time. I do find them rather messy, noisy, bad-tempered creatures. Quite loathsome, actually."

"Murdo," she persisted. "You must tell me some time about Kirstie and Miranda. How are we to be close if I know so little of that part of your life?"

He pushed his chair farther still from the table, and folded his arms against his chest. She saw this gesture for what he intended: a protective barrier to keep off her plundering. Perhaps he thought too, as she now did, of that male rib plucked out in Eden.

What did she see on his face? Anger? The beginning of a childish sulk? Or had she only imagined these reactions, for as he began to speak, his features were perfectly composed.

"My dear, let us regard my first marriage, and indeed my second, as equations that are complete in themselves. Life is not a continuous manifold but a series of quite discrete states. You and I – together – constitute just such a new state of being. All that existed previously has fallen away, like a snake shedding its skin, if you will."

She did not at all care for this image. "Murdo, I don't believe you can abstract yourself from your past with such facility. Your first two marriages are surely as much a part of you as are your children."

"Indeed," he snapped. "What exactly is it you want of me? To eat what you believe to be my soul? To dig out my very marrow with a metaphorical spoon that you call love? I will not have it, do you hear? I will not have it."

He got up so abruptly that his chair toppled on the stone floor.

Suzanne sat alone for some minutes, staring at the fallen chair. It looked like an insect flipped on its back, she thought, legs waving piteously in the air. She had failed in her resolve, just that piteously. As Murdo too, had failed.

In bed, she tossed a long time. When she did sleep, Suzanne dreamt of Gemma at work in the refuge. A long line of clients queued at the door. She thought she spied herself among them. But as the dream zoomed closer, she saw that there was only a superficial resemblance. The woman in the queue was tall and dark. Her chin-length hair swung in an immaculate arc as she looked down at the baby in her arms. But her face was not Suzanne's.

The line of waiting women dissolved. Now she lay on sun-warmed grass, a breeze with the delicacy of lace playing about her bare shoulders. The breeze sought out the tender skin of her inner wrists, her palms, the crooks of her elbows.

She woke to his scent and his heat, to the light touch of Murdo's fingertips on her flesh. She woke to Murdo, saying: "Oh, my dear, I am so sorry. I have been overwrought. Years ago, you see, I did lose a student. A dear, brave, brilliant young man."

"Like you, my sweet. Dear and brave and brilliant." His heat worked its habitual miracle, fusing their separateness. She understood that she had come home, and that her body, which underwent such indescribable pleasure with this man, could never lie. She knew her own name only because he breathed it softly over and over into her ear.

11

The Children

Suzanne woke and stretched, catlike, willing every muscle to relive the pleasure of the night before. She felt elated, as though she had been running at the edge of the sea, the salt tang making a fire in her blood. She saw that Murdo's side of the bed was empty, but this did not at all surprise her as he often rose before six a.m.

She reached out blindly for the alarm clock on the bedside table, and winced as something stabbed her thumb. Sitting up, she saw a red rose lying on top of a note with a few lines of Murdo's script. She sucked at the tiny puncture the thorn had made, and squinted to make out the minuscule letters.

"My dear – Gone to Edinburgh for an Astronomical Society meeting. Back late. Don't wait up. – M."

Well, *M*, she mused, how thoughtful of you to leave me a rose, and how careless to forget the thorn. She was quite irked. He had made no mention the day before of a meeting in Edinburgh. But of course their conversation at dinner had been barely civil. Only their lovemaking had succeeded in combing out the raggedness of the day; that silky slide of flesh into flesh, that sacrament in silence.

Recalling her pleasure, she felt ready to forgive him yet another abrupt departure. She was more and more confident that his silence would eventually yield to her.

She dressed hurriedly, determined to start work on a project to help her feel more at home with the rambling house and grounds. She would create a herbal garden, planting just a few of her mother's staples. It was not yet too late in the year and she had seen a herbalist's shop in Edinburgh where she was sure she could find the seeds she needed. For today, she would simply dig the patch, not over the ruined apothecary's garden, which was best, she thought, left as it was. But in the clearing near the creaturely outbuilding. For despite the scene with Murdo, Suzanne felt drawn to the structure's rough-hewn stone face, its hard-packed earthen floor, its living roof. She liked too, the fairy tale allure of its two identical doors, only feet apart and yet opening into the same space. Or did they? Did it really matter by which door one chose to enter?

Suzanne believed it did. Every choice mattered, the most apparently superficial having often the greatest portent. Would she wear shoes this morning, for example, or would she not?

She opted to go barefoot. And so it was that when she entered the kitchen, she did not disturb the lean grey-haired man who stood with his back to her, peering into the refrigerator. She was surprised but certainly not afraid. He did not have the aspect of a thief. There was something about his stance that declared he was in some sense, at home. And the rope-like spareness of his body, the prominent blue veins in his forearm, were all consistent with Murdo's description of Jeremy. The ascetic son. He who wears the hair shirt.

When Jeremy turned, the gaunt beauty of his face took her aback. He had the look of a fasting saint, the flesh quite scooped away at his temples and under his cheekbones. His high forehead was accentuated by his receding hairline and he wore his greying hair in a long queue as if to compensate. The long hair dramatized his natural severity and Suzanne saw he was not without vanity.

He looked her directly in the eye, a regard she read as at once calm and arrogant. He showed not the least other reaction to her presence, as if he had been all the time aware that she was there. She was uncertain whether this was indeed the case, or simply his habitual consummate self-control. For she could easily imagine his lean form ducking and diving through a rain of sniper fire, one hand grasping a small tape recorder, a steno pad in the back pocket of his jeans. She saw there was a thin white scar on his chin, in the shape of a down-turned half-circle.

She was about to speak when he addressed her in the cultivated tones so much favoured by BBC news readers. "The third Mrs. Murdo Napier, I presume." He clicked his heels together, made a stiff bow from the waist, so that she could be in no doubt she was being mocked.

"And you must be Jeremy," she responded, smiling, willing all the warmth she could into her voice. But all her attempt at conciliation garnered was a distinct glare. For Christ's sake, she wondered, whatever is wrong with the man? Is he afraid I will try to mother him, or steal his inheritance? She realized it had never occurred to her that there might even be an inheritance.

She sat down at the kitchen table, removed a crisp red apple from the fruit bowl and bit into it. To hell with him, she thought. What most disconcerted her was how attractive she would have found this Jeremy under other circumstances. He looked the kind of man who would go to the grave holding fast to his leftist principles, who exposed evils of all kinds at great risk to his own personal safety. The kind of man who was acutely aware of the inequities women suffered and who would probably contort himself so as to be sensitive and fair. Although he was apparently most disinclined to be so with her. So perhaps his resemblance to some exemplary Man of Principle was merely artificial. Perhaps, she thought with smug satisfaction, he was simply a prick.

Jeremy put out his arm and Suzanne, thinking he had softened and wanted to shake hands, extended hers across the table. But he merely grimaced and reached behind her to the china cupboard to take down a small bowl. Then he hunted noisily in the cutlery drawer for a spoon. He turned back to the refrigerator, and took out her tub of Balkan yogurt, which he spooned into the bowl.

He sat down opposite her and began to eat, fastidiously and slowly as if each spoonful had an intrinsic mysterious weight that only he could reckon. Suzanne had finished her apple, and sat watching him eat, hoping her close scrutiny would disconcert him a little. Half-way through his meal, he spoke again.

"Yours?" he asked, waving the yogurt-laded spoon in the air. "I somehow can't imagine Murdo partaking of a substance that might actually do him some good. Surely he is still enamoured of good old British beef?"

Suzanne automatically pictured Murdo standing beside his strikingly gaunt son. By contrast, he seemed florid, barrel-chested. Certainly over-indulged. She was uncomfortably aware that this was the second time this morning she had mentally slighted Murdo, so that when she spoke, her anger at Jeremy was more evident than she had intended.

"Why are you being so rude?"

He raised his eyebrows in a pantomime display of surprise, which made his long face even more censorious.

"Well, what do you expect of me?" he challenged. "Did you think I would hug you nicely and say, 'Welcome, dear step-mama'? Do you not see that would be a trifle ridiculous?"

"Is it my age?" she asked, determined to get at the pith of what irked him. "Do you find the age difference between me and Murdo offensive?"

"Oh, please." He pushed his chair back as if anxious to set his body at an angle away from hers. Then he pushed at the edge of the table with the flat of his hands so that she had the impression he had made his entire body an inverted bow. It seemed he must shoot at her.

Suzanne strove to ride and contain her mounting anger. She breathed deeply, but not so audibly that Jeremy would be aware of her efforts at self-control, "You didn't answer," she persisted. "Is it the age difference that irks you?"

"Oh, really." The look he gave her was so supercilious, he might have been carved from a block of ice. "As you Americans say – I could care less."

"I am a Canadian."

"Ah, really." He nodded with a mock sageness.

"Forgive me," he continued. "Of course, I should have realized. The Canadian style is so very distinctive." He ran the tip of his tongue over his upper lip. He almost smiled. In that ghostly warmth that played about his lips, she thought she caught a glimpse of what it might be like to have this man as a friend.

"Is this something to do with your mother?" She had been unsure how to phrase this question. Best, she thought, just to blurt it out. It was hardly as if Jeremy were being terribly subtle.

She was absolutely unprepared for the forcefulness of his reaction. He struck the table with his fist, leapt up abruptly and crossed to the window. He leant in toward it, pressing his pale forehead against the glass. He grasped the wood frame on both sides and she saw that tips of his fingers were quite white. When he turned round, his face was absolutely contorted, whether by hatred or anger she could not tell. She was heartily sorry that she had probed such a rawness in him. She half stood, uncertain whether to cross the room and put her hand on his shoulder.

He raised his hand to gesture her away. She could see the outline of his ribs rising and falling under his T-shirt.

"What do you know of my mother?" His tone made this an accusation, rather than a question. He began to pace between the sink and the window, his hands thrust deep in his pockets, his back a little bent, as if he might suddenly cave in on himself.

"I know very little of your mother," she responded, whether he wished an answer or not. She had sat down again, unwilling to leave him alone, despite his abrasiveness with her. She saw him flinch every so often, a slight tremor pass through his shoulders. She wondered if he might very recently have been under fire. Bosnia, she remembered Murdo saying, although he had seemed then to be merely speculating.

He raised his head to look at her and stopped pacing. She saw his spine stiffen, as if some core of memory were rising in him, hardening him. His eyes narrowed, turned the perturbed grey of a rain-laden sky.

"Did you know that he plucked her from the convent, that she was just eighteen, about to take her vows? That way, you see, he was ensured a virgin. He had some cockeyed theory that the female virgin was a living manifestation of pure number. But no doubt he has confided all his cherished little notions to you?" He grimaced, twisted his bony hands together.

Talk to the children, Gemma had advised. And here she was, sitting in a room with Murdo's son. An angry, brittle, attractive man who quite evidently loathed his father. Suzanne thought of the cruel measurements noted in the pathetic journal, with all its horrific implications that a young mother had been deliberately separated from her baby. She felt sick hearing Jeremy's substantiation of what she most feared. What if the suffering that had drawn her to Murdo was in fact an abiding guilt? What if he continued to agonize over his treatment of Miranda after she had given birth? What if he had indeed mentally tortured her with the unrealistic demand that she recapture the form of a virgin girl? Could she herself forgive him if all this were true? Even if it were something he had done thirty or more years ago?

Suzanne longed to question Jeremy directly about Miranda, and about his relationship with Murdo. Yet even had Jeremy not been so obviously resistant, she still felt it would be inappropriate to go behind Murdo's back. On the other hand, her lingering suspicions might drive out love.

She was about to speak when Jeremy turned on her again. "The Virgin is one of your own pet topics, I understand. You had some success with a picture book, I believe."

You condescending git, she thought. Are you deliberately trying to rile me, or simply get away from the subject of Miranda?

"Is that what you have against me?" she asked. "Do you find my work specious?"

"Specious? No. Self-indulgent? Yes. I am frankly amazed at how the feminist book industry manages to proliferate. Your brand of literature is all very well for middle-class women going through minor psychic turbulence. Just plunder the ancient box of archetypes, pull out a picture and try it on. Virgin? Wise old Crone? Whore? Whatever makes you feel better about your already pampered self."

"It reminds me," he continued, and again his tongue traced his upper lip, "of those colourful band-aids one can buy for toddlers, with pictures of storybook animals or wretched Mickey Mouse. Stick it on dear, and you'll feel ever so much better."

"But just tell me. What good does your pseudo-intellectual feminism do for the woman in the Gaza Strip who is haggard and febrile at forty from giving birth to fifteen children? Because her husband demands she be a birth machine. Producing offspring, proving his virility through the medium of his wife's ravaged body. This is the sole power he can demonstrate to his peers, in a world where everything else has been stripped away from him. He maintains his self-respect by begetting. That poor, suffering creature who is his wife, what do your pretty picture books do for her? Or your book on holy whores? You want to go to Calcutta and see those lovely young girls sold into prostitution by their families. Swallowing little vials of coloured water that they purchase from charlatans who tell them it will protect them from AIDS. And then these young women confidently lie down, ten to twenty times a day, with the scum of the earth. Where, in the name of heaven, is the holiness in that?"

"Do you think I am so naive?" she exploded. "Do you think I am blind to the horrors of the world? Or that I am exploitative in the way I make my living? Or that I am…"

"Self-serving?" he broke in. "Yes. Yes. I do. I believe you are all those things. And most especially self-serving. And please don't tell me these little nostrums you propagate are going to filter through human consciousness, or through the airwaves, or through the spectra, or whatever it is you people believe."

The tip of his tongue darted out again, and she thought how disgustingly reptilian he looked, and how terribly smug. She was furious in part because she could not refute the truth of his accusation. His was an argument that she frequently conducted silently with herself, and aloud with Gemma. What good exactly did her books do? Yet she was certainly not going to expose her doubts to this man in this context. But at least, she could use his tirade to get to the root of the immediate problem.

"Is this why you dislike me on sight?" she confronted him. "Is it because of my books?"

"Dislike you! I don't dislike you. I despise you. Because you have married a monster. And that makes you either as vile as he, or a complete fool."

"Jeremy!" The voice had the bracing purity of wind chimes. The sound seemed miraculously to clear the room of its vitriol. Suzanne turned to see a fairy standing in the kitchen doorway. Or such was the image the young woman projected, in part because she had so speedily transformed the atmosphere. She was about five feet tall and ethereally slim in a sleeveless, ankle-length pink cotton shift. She looked as if she had very recently bathed her face with rose petals. Her feet were bare. Her pale gold hair swung across her face as she flung herself into Jeremy's arms.

"Clara," she heard Jeremy murmur from under the muffle of the young woman's embrace. The top of her head came just under his chin. Then she tipped her head back and put her finger lightly to the scar under his bottom lip.

"Oh, my poor Jeremy," she cried softly, then kissed his face. "However did it happen?"

"A camera, believe it or not, my sweet. Our jeep hit a land mine. We were all thrown clear, fortunately. Just a few cuts and bad bruises. My camera flipped up and sliced me, as you can see."

"Oh Jeremy." She hugged him tightly. "I do wish you'd get a safer job."

"And go mad with restlessness and guilt. No thanks."

They stood apart, hands linked, gazing at each other. One might take them for lovers, Suzanne thought. Families remained a foreign land for her. She viewed them still, as she had since a child, through glass. The lighted windows she passed on her way home to Ada. Five bodies ranged on a sofa watching television, seven round a table busily eating. One child screaming at another, while a mother intervened. Even a family of three seemed to her so very many, compared to the two-in-one that was Suzanne and Ada. From the impassioned tales her school friends told of their home life, Suzanne gleaned that families were a mesh of stresses and counter stresses, a world of ever-shifting alliances and nodes of power, where sibling rivalry flared daily or hourly. Where one was arbitrarily assigned a role one must wear though it choked like a dog collar. The Pretty One. The Clever One. The One with the Temper. The Musical One.

She had perceived that for a family, no transaction was trivial. Everything had import. The spilling of milk, the struggle over a wishbone, a mistimed compliment, the unreasonable demand – anything at all might reorder the ever-changing factions. Families, she thought, shared the instability of tectonic plates. One's character was fired in that furnace, and with much pain.

Whereas it seemed to her that she had grown up beside Ada, like a sturdy plant, in conditions her mother fostered just as naturally. All dissension had been outside: the jibes of prurient neighbours or the clucking tongues of the women's church group.

If she had missed anything, she thought, it was not a paternal presence, but what she now beheld in the eyes of Jeremy and Clara. Brother-sister love sustained by the bonds of blood. These two shared a father, but not a mother. And where was Murdo? Why had he not told her they were coming? Because Clara also believed her father to be a monster?

"When did you get in, sweetie?" Jeremy asked.

"After midnight," Clara replied. "And you?"

"Oh, tenish."

Suzanne realized that she and Murdo had then been in bed making love. The bed springs squeaked quite noticeably, so that Jeremy might well have been aware that his father was having sex with his new wife. But the most pertinent question was whether Murdo knew that Jeremy was in the house.

"Did you see him?" Clara asked, her bell-pure tone quavering slightly.

"No, my dear." He stroked Clara's hair. "We skirted each other. Neither of us has lost the ability to sniff each other out at a distance, thank God. He left me a note."

"He left you a note!"

The two women spoke at once. Suzanne was aware that it was she who sounded most surprised. Clara's tone was in fact far more wry. As if to say, "Well, Murdo leaves notes the way animals leave droppings."

As soon as Suzanne spoke, Clara made a little leap into the middle of the kitchen so that she stood equidistant between her and Jeremy. She moved with a balletic grace that was absolutely unfaltering. Yet Suzanne perceived an underlying wilful drama in the young woman's movements. Clara gestured so liberally with her hands that her address struck Suzanne as artificially staged.

"Now, really," she began, "you two must shake hands and start again." Clara was a pantomime fairy, darting on her toes, now toward Suzanne, now toward Jeremy. An actress, Suzanne decided, for every one of Clara's gestures seemed hyperbolic, magnified, then held in time those few instants longer than necessary. And the fluting voice, with its flawless enunciation, might well be cultivated through hours of practice, and not simply another gift nature had bestowed on an exquisite young woman.

Clara flung her arms around her brother's neck. Suzanne heard her whisper: "It's not her fault, Jeremy. It's only that she hasn't seen yet how truly horrible he is."

Suzanne felt a chill ride up her spine as Clara echoed Jeremy's judgement. Was Murdo indeed the heartless puppet master that Miranda's journal implied? Apart from a few fits of pique, his behaviour in her presence had never been less than irreproachable. When was this legendary cruelty to begin manifesting itself? Or had it perhaps already begun, in forms too subtle for her to recognize?

A wave of sick paranoia engulfed her. It took all her concentration to stave off the fear. There was a kind of contamination in the air still, spread by nasty winged things she knew she could banish if she concentrated her thoughts. Visualize, Suzanne. She imagined a wind laden with salt to sweep the room quite clean. The effort made her close her eyes.

When she opened them, Clara had once again claimed centre stage on the kitchen's flagstone floor. Again she stood on tiptoe, arms fluttering, her face a bright star. Then, in a twinkling, she was transformed, her animation extinguished, her lithe body apparently slack and formless. A most cunning illusion, reflected Suzanne, grateful to be removed for a second from thoughts of Murdo. But as soon as Clara spoke, she saw she should have realized all too well, just where this latest pantomime was going.

"I do him sometimes as a gobbling whale." Clara's piping, childlike tone made her cruelly comic characterization of Murdo's dejection all the more cutting. Suzanne fought the urge to stop up her ears.

"I'm in a children's theatre troupe," Clara told Suzanne. "Itinerant. We have three caravans. One for the costumes and sets and two for us. And sometimes," she rushed on, "I do him as a greedy lion, swallowing down the sun. He tries to take our light, you know."

Suzanne sat listening to this condemnation of Murdo by metaphor, stunned, still a little sick. Would they announce next that she had married a murderer? Even making allowances for Clara's ingrained histrionics, her sincerity seemed unquestionable. Underneath the strained unreality of this encounter, Suzanne could not evade the deeper questions. If she truly loved Murdo, would she doubt him?

Meanwhile, Jeremy sat nodding silently at his sister's performance, smiling beneficently, his eyes crinkling in affection. Suzanne saw two loving conspirators, delighting in a mockery of the man to whom she had bound herself. The problem was that she found herself instinctively drawn to both these people, which made their perception of Murdo all the more perturbing.

She had a fleeting and ludicrous vision of herself as peacemaker, smoothing out the familial discord as a good housekeeper would tug out the rucks in a linen tablecloth. Yet she sensed their rupture with Murdo was irredeemable.

She took an almost guilty pleasure at Clara and Jeremy's startled look when she posed her blunt question: "Why exactly do you dislike your father so?"

"Oh, please," said Jeremy, turning on her the deliberately supercilious glare. "Please do not use that wretched word."

"We just call him Murdo," Clara explained. "Or sometimes pater. To call him father implies a bond that is simply not there, you see."

"But what is it he does, or has done to you?" Suzanne persisted.

"Oh, for God's sake," Jeremy snapped. "Stick around and you'll find out, won't you. But I'll give you a clue. He puts absolutely no brakes on his will to power. He has to control everything in his immediate reality. This means you," he said, pointing a bony finger at Suzanne. "And it would mean me and Clara and Callum if we let him get near us. Then he'd pin us in place on his godawful mathematical grid, or whatever he calls the choking strictures he puts on his world. And, it's as Clara said, he will swallow your light, extinguish you."

"But why on earth do you come to visit, if you hate him so?" What was she hoping to hear, a softening of attitude, a recantation?

"Oh, we don't come for him," Clara announced, with one of her charming little bounds across the floor. "We come for our mothers' sake. They are both buried here, you see. We come to be with them and with each other. The three of us, you see."

"But how do you avoid Murdo while you are here?" Suzanne asked, falling into the fatalism that apparently characterized this family's relations.

"Oh," Clara began and then ceased abruptly, a look of concern momentarily shadowing her features. She came and sat then, close to Suzanne. "He's never here when we're here, you see. It's a kind of longstanding tacit agreement. We come, for a week or so, and he goes. He didn't tell you, did he?"

Suzanne was conscious of the purity of Clara's breath as she spoke. She smelled of almonds and of violets. She recalled another of Ada's lessons. If you are confused about someone's true intentions or true character, seek your answer in their breath. At eleven, Suzanne had asked for clarification. Well, you pay attention to the rhythm of the person's breathing, Ada explained. Does it seem at all caught or forced when he or she speaks? And the smell too. Not, she added, is it oniony or garlicky? But only does it seem right and natural? For duplicity will stink in all ways, Ada said. In this household, Suzanne reasoned, these were instructions she must always be putting into practice.

Clara smells of almonds and violets. Her concern for my feelings seems quite genuine. But she is an actress by profession – albeit one dedicated to the pantomime and large gestures. And most well-to-do British families had a great penchant for playing games, did they not? Idiosyncratic games that were founded on the strengths and foibles of each player, where a daggered word might be sheathed in love, where you learned the secret code or perished (emotionally, at least). Were these two drawing her into a game for their own amusement? Was it time to play "Punish the presumptuous stepmother?" Or were they simply telling the truth as they saw it?

"I will leave you two a while, I think." Suzanne registered the kindness in Jeremy's voice rather than the actual words. If he and Clara were being cunning, describing a Murdo who did not actually exist, would they have built sensitivity into their little scenario?

"He is the sweetest man you could ever meet," Clara said, as soon as Jeremy was out of the room. "Without him,

I do really wonder if Callum and I would have survived. You would see Jeremy's goodness for yourself, if only you had not done this stupid thing."

"Clara," Suzanne began, drawing her spine as erect as possible, so that when she spoke she was looking down into the girl's face. And why not, she thought. Why not use her six inches of extra height to her own advantage? Why not use anything to help her surmount this situation that seemed to grow more murky and perilous with each passing second? "Clara, what stupid thing do you think I have done?"

"Why... marrying Murdo, of course. I meant marrying Murdo. I mean, why on earth did you do it? I read your book on the Virgin, you see, and I was so impressed. I mean about virginity being a state of mind and not something men can take from us, or sell, or make us feel guilty if our hymen happens to be broken."

"Like those lovely paintings you describe that Bonnard did of his wife, drying herself with a towel, or looking down so contentedly at her own naked body in the bath. He could see that pure girlish aspect of herself that she had kept, despite intercourse and childbirth. We can keep that virgin sense of ourselves, always."

"And that idea, I mean, your book, was such a help to a friend of mine who was raped. That's why, you see, I was so shocked when I heard it was you he had married. We all knew he was bound to do it again some time. Marry, I mean. But I suppose we had all imagined someone rather more acquiescent. I still don't understand how you..."

"Clara, Clara, please stop a minute." Because really, thought Suzanne, you must give me a little space to breathe and think and to look into your eyes and see that – yes, they do seem clear and guileless. "Clara, tell me – specifically – what is wrong between you and your fa... between you and Murdo. He is wilful. He tries to take your light, you say. But what has he actually done to the three of you?"

"And to our mothers," Clara said quietly, looking down at her bare feet.

"What?" Suzanne demanded. "Just tell me, please."

Clara leapt up. "I'm sorry," she said. "Jeremy wrote me about what we could tell you, but we decided we must wait until Callum gets here. I mean, we cannot talk to you without Callum because in many ways – apart from our mothers – he suffered the most because of Murdo. So please, wait until Callum comes. And then we'll tell you everything."

The girl was moving toward the kitchen door, obviously anxious to get away. Then she reached out and touched Suzanne's shoulder. "Callum will be here in a day or two. I'm sure of it."

"And until then, you will leave me hanging," Suzanne said, more vehemently than she intended, for Clara immediately withdrew her hand.

The young woman took a deep breath, as if readying herself for making some revelation. Or recitation, Suzanne wondered.

"I can tell you," Clara began, her words coming slower now, "about an incident with Murdo that involves you."

"Go on," Suzanne encouraged, injecting a confidence into her tone she did not in fact feel.

"Do you remember about a year or so ago, one of the quality Sunday papers did a profile on you in their magazine section?"

Suzanne nodded. Her publisher had arranged the interview, and had been pleased with the result. Suzanne had not read the article herself, having too often experienced frustration at how the press twisted or demeaned her work. Gemma had read it, she recalled, and told her the piece was quite balanced. She recalled Gemma passing her the magazine for a quick look. Suzanne had been struck by the photograph of herself, so much so that she did not even glance at the text. For what she saw in the imperious upward tilt of the chin, the gold hoop earring shining against her dark hair, and the strong three-quarter profile, was an image of her mother. Suzanne was not much given to looking in mirrors, at least not for long. She had been blessed with good health and looks that were naturally dramatic, and she was grateful. But she saw no point in hunting her own mirror image for incipient crow's feet or errant eyebrow hair. She was careful to avoid any such obsessiveness, and thus she had simply been oblivious to how she had changed in her early thirties.

"Murdo sent me that article about you, along with a horrid little note," Clara said. "I have a post office box in York, you see. I don't know how he got my address, but he did. When I saw his writing on the envelope, I really didn't want to open it. But then I thought, perhaps something had happened to Jeremy, and I hadn't realized. Because we generally do know what's happening with each other just through the air, you see, especially Callum and I because we're twins."

"So, foolishly, I opened it and there was this article about you and your books and that glamorous photo and then his nasty little note tumbled out too. – Dear Belle, he wrote – he calls me Belle because he knows I hate it – Have you read anything by this extremely attractive feminist? And mustn't her sisters with their size 46 dungarees absolutely detest her. I'll bet she makes the sheets churn and burn. Fancy her for a stepmother, dearest Belle? Shall I inflame the whore in the feminist?"

Suzanne felt someone had just anaesthetized her. She looked at Clara, who regarded her so very earnestly, and not without pain.

"You must believe me," Clara said. "Why on earth would I make it up? And he is that terribly vulgar, you see. Vulgarly dirty-minded. I don't mean just about sex. But he has to pull everything down to his level, so that he can control you, as Jeremy said."

"When?" Suzanne asked. "Clara, when did he send you the note with the article?"

"Oh," she said. "Shortly after it came out."

"A good six months before I even met him then?"

"About a year and a half ago, yes."

"So you are saying he had selected me as a prospective marriage partner before he even met me?"

"Not prospective, no. He had definitely fixed on you as his next coup. He wanted to bring the glamorous feminist to heel."

"And then what? Bring me to heel and make me what, Clara?"

The girl shrugged but without petulance. The gesture was more as if she threw off some fetid piece of clothing. Then she said: "I think it is best if neither of us ever know. You must leave him, don't you see?"

Suzanne could take no more. She ran out of the kitchen and down the passageway and out the front door. She ran as she had not run since she was a girl. The words in her head were not her own, for she could find none at that moment to match the turmoil inside her.

The words were Isobel Gowdie's, whose trial she had recently read an account of. "I shall go into a hare with sorrow and sighing and meikle care. And I shall go in the Devil's name, Aye, till I come home again."

Poor Isobel, Suzanne thought. Poor Isobel. You wanted to get away from those men who hounded you, the inquisitors, the torturers, the upstanding men of the kirk, and James VI himself who never missed a witch trial if he could help it. You would be a hare to escape their hounding. The Devil had nothing to do with it.

12

Mathematical Drills

Suzanne lay on her back in the warm grass near the out-building where she had first lifted the lamp to the picture of the baby Jeremy. She was out of breath from running, her stomach soured by what she had heard. If only Murdo were here to state his own case. She shrugged off the paranoid notion that he had arranged the children's attack on him as a test of her love. So it had come to this pass, she thought glumly, where her perceptions twisted and clotted, like the mess of knots she always pictured when she heard the word *imbroglio*.

She sought solace in the drifting cloudscape, ready as a child to spy out shapes. Here was a massive continent splitting asunder. The skeleton of a fish held the sun briefly in its ribcage, before disintegrating suddenly into wisps of sea spume. Then, there was a dragon, rearing in profile against the blue. She could make out each spine on its thorny back and the dense webbing between its claws.

This aerial dragon spurred a recollection of a ritual with Ada she had not thought of for years. They lay side by side in the long grass of their tiny fenced backyard. (Ada did not possess a lawnmower and besides, she delighted in the flow of the shining green under wind and sun.) Ada held her hand, and silently they watched the procession of white forms, at first so high above her, and gradually, it seemed to Suzanne, under and even inside her. Every so often Ada would grip her hand tightly and ask in a tone earnest and hushed: "Do you see them? There! The dragon veins." She waved a red-nailed finger and Suzanne strove to see the curved channels that conducted cosmic vitality to the earth. And vice-versa. For as above, so below, said the most basic precept of the Wicca.

Sometimes Suzanne did actually see the dragon veins – most often, when she was not striving to do so. Like insight, which her mother had in abundance, these visions were a gift. Once or perhaps twice, in her twenties, Suzanne had seen the entire physical world streaming away into light, so that birch trees were fronds of white-gold energy, and the solid earth beneath her a luminous sea. At the very point of merging with this unceasing flow, she grew fearful and closed her eyes. When she opened them again, the familiar solidity of the world had returned, bark quite surely delineated from earth, and each rock sturdy in its own separateness. She experienced then an almost numbing sense of loss and a fumbling awareness that she had somehow failed. Whether this failure had to do with a lack of courage, or a refusal to surrender herself, she was unclear. She had, she supposed, an abiding anxiety that if she persisted in these moments of exalted transport, she risked either madness or death.

Ada had no such fears. And of course, Ada would have seen through all the murk to the essential plot of the Napier family. She had an uncanny ability to spy out lies and self-deception. I have the disadvantage, thought Suzanne, of being blinded by love. Or was she? For in the light of his children's accusations, her mental image of Murdo had become undeniably tarnished. What if Gemma were right, and she not fallen in love with a man at all, but with a pro-jected image of that man? What if she had fallen in love with what she took to be his life story? And now even that compelling narrative might prove to be false.

There was nothing she could do but wait to hear all sides. Wait for Callum; then wait for Murdo.

She had a sudden urge to look again at the photographs of Miranda. She leapt to her feet and pushed open the same door of the outbuilding she had used on her first visit. To her amazement, the interior was already lit. The oil lamp was gleaming on the table where she had previously found the boxes with Miranda's puppets and the two photographs. The boxes were gone. Had Murdo taken them? But who had lit the lamp? Had Jeremy or Clara already been here this morning? Why would they leave a lamp burning?

Suzanne bent down to look beneath the table, where all was cradled gloom. She began to feel about on the earthen floor, but stopped when she smelled the unmistakable mustiness of mouse droppings. As she stood up, she heard something stirring in the loft. She turned sharply on her heel and saw flecks of straw floating down. Whatever had made the disturbance was definitely larger than a mouse or a rat.

"Is anyone there?" Had her voice quavered? If there was only one, she knew she could down an attacker within seconds. If there were two, she would be in trouble. She was certainly far enough away from the house that neither Jeremy nor Clara would hear her call.

He came down from the loft in a single bound. Suzanne staggered back; then immediately put herself on alert. He was young, extremely grimy, and rake thin in a T-shirt that was more holes than cloth and much-patched jeans. Oddly, he stayed crouched, like an ape, his arms dangling. Suzanne's whole body was tensed. She was uncertain whether to run, yet his atavistic posture, the black streaks on his face, and the fixed stare of his unmatched eyes (one was an opaque, dead blue) kept her rooted where she stood. The young man too, stayed absolutely still, holding his crouched position.

"What are you doing here?" she asked, striving to make her tone kind and non-challenging. For she feared he might be mad, or one of the lost children who these days took to the roads, lived in trees, took the names of ancient British tribes, sometimes even painted themselves with woad. Suzanne very much admired the young members of the ecological tribes, who put their half-naked bodies in the path of bulldozers in often vain attempts to stop the destruction of parklands, razed to make another sullen, clogged motorway. But some, like this one perhaps, were just solitary wanderers, haunting the edges of free festivals, taking bad drugs.

"Poor boy," she nearly said aloud, for she understood she had no reason to fear him. He was so fragile, the straw clinging to his blond curls, his ribs showing through the riddled T-shirt. But even as she formed the words in her mind, he was circling her in a grotesque, shambling dance, as if she were the fire and he the worshipper.

"Stop it!" To her relief, he obeyed, stopping directly in front of her. Now, however, he assumed a grovelling position, like a chastised dog, his head cocked, an expectant, curious look in his unsettling eyes.

"Zoobly," he said. "Mowkran howstater crack gum."

And again: "Zoobly." He lay flat on his belly, and stroked her bare feet under her sandals. "Zoobly," he said, as she jerked away from him, shocked at how disturbingly erotic was his touch. She had to fight hard against the desire to bend down and take him in her arms, stroke his straw-littered hair.

"Callum!" It was Clara standing in the doorway. "I felt you were here," she trilled, running up to the young man, who was on his feet now. As his features composed, Suzanne became aware of his striking resemblance to Clara. The twins embraced. Clara burbled in his ear. "Were you being naughty with Suzanne, you silly boy? Oh Callum, I've missed you so."

He pointed to Suzanne. "Is she my new mother?" This was delivered in a ludicrous stage whisper. His eyes were wide in mock amazement.

My God, thought Suzanne, is everyone in this family a ham? Then: It's Callum and he can speak perfectly well, and why was he making a fool of me?

"Don't be silly, Callum." Clara hugged her brother tightly. "She married Murdo," she said in a kind of confiding aside that also struck Suzanne as slightly censorious. It sounded much as if she had said: Suzanne has done something stinking in the corner.

She was tempted once again just to walk away from this trio of idiosyncratic individuals. Just go away and come back to Murdo after they had decamped, with all their trickery and their theatrics. Callum came up to her and Suzanne tensed. If he speaks gibberish at me, she decided, I will slap his face.

"You are so pretty," he said. "Why have you done this stupid thing?"

Suzanne was absolutely nonplussed. She could read nothing teasing or false in his face. His eyes were level with hers. The opaque one, she saw now, was blind.

Clara was chattering again, pulling at Callum's arm. "Did you drive that bike of yours all the way from London? You're disgustingly dirty. Go give Jeremy a kiss and then have a bath."

"Will she bathe me?" he asked with a wink and a sly little smile at Suzanne.

"Callum!" Clara did this time look genuinely irritated. She gave her brother a cuff under the chin that just crossed the borderline of playful.

"Sorry," he said. "That was quite out of line." He included both Clara and then Suzanne in his apology, turning his head round so that he could look at her with his one good eye.

"Suzanne wants to know about us and Murdo," Clara told him, her face so serious that Suzanne saw what she would be at fifty. "We said we would talk when you came."

"Ugh!" he said and collapsed on the floor in a sorrowful heap.

"Oh, get up, Callum. You know we have to do this. It would be unthinkable to leave her to his devices."

He stood up, sent Suzanne a lugubrious look, and nodded.

"Yes," he said. "The thing is you see," he spoke now to Suzanne, "I hate him so that it is intensely painful for me to speak about him at all." He put his index finger to his temple and twisted it as if he were inserting a long spiralling screw.

"It's true," Clara said. "Callum has just cause." It unsettled Suzanne to see the twins' faces turned pinched and white about the eyes and nostrils. This cannot possibly be an act, she thought. Then again, dissembling was Clara's craft, and Callum had feigned madness well enough.

Callum made a deep bow. "I am," he said, "the Pater Hater."

Clara merely looked at him; then hugged herself as if a shadow passed over the sun and she found the day quite spoiled.

"It means a sacrifice," she said quietly, looking at Suzanne.

"Yes," Suzanne responded. "I understand." Certainly she was beginning to accept completely that their loathing of Murdo was unshiftable. Whatever came to pass, there would be nothing she could do toward reconciling the children with the father.

She watched Clara and Callum amble away together through the trees. Abruptly, the girl bumped her brother with her hip. Then they were off and racing down a row of stiffly planted conifers. The sun was high. The trees' shadows struck the path like a line of individual spears. So that it seemed to Suzanne they ran a gauntlet of hurtful points.

Pater Hater, he had said. So that was the *P. H.* carved so often and with such force into the oak of the bathroom cabinet. Just like Clara minutes before, Suzanne felt suddenly extremely chilled. She wrapped her arms about herself, like an imaginary breastplate, and began walking to the house, following – but much more slowly – the same shadowy path as the twins.

Jeremy, Clara, and Suzanne sat at one end of the long dining room table, Jeremy at the head, the women on either side. Callum had not yet appeared.

Suzanne faced the wall-wide claret velvet curtain, with its heavy sculpted folds. Like a cloak hiding an obscene secret, she thought, half imagining some slight stirring in its stolid drapery.

As she stared, a ghostly face emerged from the curtain's central part. A young man's face, pale and finely shaped, softly gleaming in the gloom. Suzanne went cold but did not make a sound. Which was just as well. For when Callum stepped forth, washed and wearing a clean dark blue shirt and jeans, his brother and sister simply nodded, as though they had all along known he was standing behind the curtain. Another of their self-indulgent family games? They hovered just this side of being disgustingly precious, she reflected angrily. Yet she registered their cohesion, and sensed an invisible force she took to be love.

Callum sat down beside his twin, settling in the chair with an unstudied grace. Together, he and Clara looked like angels. Jeremy, of course, was God. She was the outrider, the visiting floating spirit.

Callum had thrown his head back and was running his fingers through the tight springs of his just shampooed hair. Now he was clean, Suzanne could see how exquisite he was. His apparent vulnerability frightened her. His fully exposed throat was so slender and white. Yet she doubted that this pose was premeditated. His gestures seemed far less calculated than Clara's. Suzanne reassured herself that Callum's intent was not to make her feel guilty. This was not the sacrificial lamb exposing its windpipe; only a young man, restless and perturbed.

"Shall we begin?" said Jeremy, rapping his knuckles on the table top.

Callum moaned.

"We'll keep it brief, Callum, I promise. If at any point, this process becomes unbearable, we'll simply stop. Right?"

Clara and Callum nodded in unison. Suzanne noted that Callum's lips were pressed so tight they were virtually bloodless.

"And Suzanne," Jeremy inclined his head toward her ever so slightly. "I would ask that you keep any questions until we three have finished what we feel we can tell you today. And correspondingly, that we have the right to question you about…"

"Why you did this very stupid thing," Callum chimed in, his face lugubrious as a pantomime clown's.

"Quite," said Jeremy. "I think it best if we begin somewhere other than with the mothers. Suggestions? Boarding schools?"

Callum groaned. "Primes," he said.

"All right, then," said Jeremy, laying his hands on the table. "Primes, it is."

It was Clara who noticed Suzanne's perplexity. "Mathematical drills," she clarified. "We all had to do them before breakfast, but Murdo always gave Callum the hardest questions."

"A prime," she added, "is a number that is only divisible by one and itself."

Callum was sitting ramrod straight. His cheeks were flushed. His good eye rolled upward. He banged the table with his fist.

"Callum Napier," he intoned. "Is one million, three thousand and thirty-four a prime? Fifteen seconds, boy." His take on Murdo's inflection struck Suzanne as uncomfortably accurate.

"No?" Callum continued in his father's voice. "Dunce of a boy. To the study with you. Get in position." Callum put his head in his hands. "Bastard," Suzanne heard him murmur in his own voice. "Fucking bastard." When he emerged from behind the barrier of his interlocked fingers, he looked ready to weep.

Jeremy and Clara exchanged a look of concern. Clara put her hand on Callum's shoulder. Jeremy said quietly: "Callum, would you like a whisky? Clara, would you get the decanter and four glasses, please."

Clara walked (no fairy-light skipping this time, Suzanne noted) to the liquor cabinet and fetched Murdo's cut-glass decanter of single malt and the glasses. She poured them each a generous measure.

Suzanne did not usually drink alcohol until after sundown, but since she was the reason this ordeal was taking place, she thought it best to join in. Besides she might well need a good stiff shot in order to hear the children's stories.

"Callum?" Clara was gently stroking the back of her brother's neck.

"Sorry," he said. "I'm just not able at the moment."

"Shall I tell her then?" Clara asked.

"Yes," he said, but so softly the word seemed to Suzanne like a ghost of a breath.

Suzanne lifted the heavy glass to her lips and took a good gulp of whisky. She was terrified she was about to hear some horrendous story of sexual abuse. She realized Jeremy was watching her. He shook his head slightly. Suzanne thought he mouthed the words, "No not that." This greatly relieved her. He is a wonder, she thought, marvelling at the swiftness of his understanding.

"Murdo used to beat Callum badly whenever he failed the primes test," Clara began. "He had a switch that he used to beat him on his bare buttocks. Often until he bled. He made Callum dress up formally for these beatings. He had to wear his white shirt and tie and regulation trousers they gave him at boarding school. This only happened in the summer holidays," she added. "The rest of the time we were all sent away to school."

"Thank God for that," Suzanne managed to say. She felt quite ill, and was further upset to see that both Callum and Clara were crying.

"Shall I take over for a bit, twins?" Jeremy asked. "Callum, would you like to go outside for a while?"

"I'm all right, Jeremy. Really. It's only," he said, looking at Suzanne, "that we try not to dredge it up."

"I'm so terribly sorry," said Suzanne, painfully aware how lame this sounded.

"You are not responsible for the fact that Murdo Napier is a monster," Jeremy said. "We three sense you are a decent human being. Otherwise, we would not be telling you these things."

"The problem is that the man simply lacks all natural affections. I have no interest," he went on, "in analyzing why this is the case. He has done far too much damage for me to bother applying any disinterested compassion. As I think I told you, he was uxorious in a perverse manner. He hated me from birth, for the simple fact that I diverted Miranda's attention from him. He solved that problem by making sure she saw as little of me as possible. Effectively, he deprived a new mother of her child for his own selfish purposes. The rationale was that her health was too delicate; that she did not have the strength to breastfeed and nurture her own child."

"He was obsessed with her body, as he was later with Kirstie's, but for quite other reasons, as you will see later. As I think I told you in my outburst, for which I apologize,

Miranda was a virgin when they married, and I believe he was pathologically fixated on her virginal appearance. It was not that childbirth ruined her figure. But she had put on a little weight, which according to my maternal grandmother and my nanny, she very much needed to do in any case. And naturally there would have been stretch marks."

"But just as with Callum and the primes, Murdo had the highly irrational notion that only sheer perfection – as defined by him, of course – was good enough. He put Miranda on a strict diet that imperilled her physical health. She was already despondent at being separated from her baby. Murdo exacerbated matters by subjecting her to a ludicrous regime of weighings and measurements. She was so very young. I suppose she simply accepted his sick idea of what love was."

"My God!" Suzanne exclaimed.

"What?" Jeremy's eyes were inquisitorial, the eyes of the reporter trained to spy out information withheld.

"I found Miranda's diary," Suzanne confessed.

All three children regarded her very sharply indeed.

"And you thought what?" Jeremy challenged. "That these were the delusions of a deranged woman?"

"I…" She faltered.

"I understand," he said. "That is what you wished to believe."

She nodded. What she felt was a great sense of shame. For she realized that – yes, she had clung to the notion that the journal was indeed the ramblings of a woman ill and overwrought.

"Where exactly did you find this journal?" Jeremy asked.

"On the upper floor. In a drawer in an otherwise empty chest."

"In an otherwise empty room, I suppose."

"Yes. Virtually."

"Ah," he said, nodding at Callum and Clara, who leant together, shoulders touching, as if huddling against a bitter

wind. "We rarely venture up there, you see. We'll come to the
reasons for that later, shall we, twins?"

Clara and Callum nodded forlornly. "More whisky,
please, Clara," said Callum.

Clara topped up all four glasses.

Suzanne did not protest. I shall be quite drunk, she
thought. I shall probably need to be quite drunk. Was it
really any comfort that they at least did not accuse Murdo
of sexual abuse? Was it not sufficiently heinous that he had
regularly and brutally beaten his son, taken obscene control
of his young wife's body, and apparently hastened her
death?

Jeremy continued in his measured, priestly tones, answer-
ing her unasked question. "Miranda developed ovarian can-
cer. It wasn't caught in time and of course her immune
system had been devastated by Murdo's regime for the
recovery of her supposedly perfect form. When I was old
enough to grasp the truth of the matter, I was given the facts
of Miranda's decline by my maternal grandmother. Her story
was corroborated by my nanny. They were both powerless to
stop what was happening or perhaps they realized too late.
My grandmother never forgave herself. But, you see, Murdo
has the cunning persuasiveness of all heartless people."

"It's his lust for control, you understand," said Clara. Her
arm circled Callum's shoulders. "I think it's related to the
mathematics. He wants to reduce the world to a set of chilling equations. You know, like that horrible time-space net he
talks about with all its nasty little nodules. When I was
younger, I used to have nightmares of being tangled up in
that net, choking with its cords in my mouth and around my
throat and my body all contorted and twisting in the webbing. But that relates too, to how he killed our mother."
Here, she hugged Callum harder.

"Can you manage this, Callum?" Jeremy asked gently.
"We can stop now if you wish."

Callum drank down a good inch of whisky. "A bit more's okay, I think."

"Just say the word, Callum," Jeremy reassured him.

Suzanne took another sip of whisky. Without the alcohol, she thought, we would all find this quite unbearable.

"It was Murdo who encouraged our mother to get interested in hang gliding," Clara began. "She was very strong and at school she excelled at gymnastics. Her instructor said she had a natural state of suspension. When she jumped hurdles, she seemed to hang a few seconds in the air above them. She would tell us this, you know, when we were little and we would say – 'Well, Mummy, it's because you're an angel.'"

Callum shuddered.

"And she was, you see," Clara continued, "all the things Murdo was not. Warm, affectionate, funny, kind. We had her until we were eleven. In that way, I suppose, we were luckier than Jeremy because he didn't really know Miranda at all. To have real memories of her, I mean."

"I think Kirstie enjoyed the hang gliding at first. But Murdo was always pushing her to take more risks. He didn't participate in the sport, of course. He was the observer. He stayed on the ground, making his horrid little notes, drawing his wretched diagrams of the arcs she made in the air."

Suzanne's stomach lurched, as she recalled the incomprehensible diagrams she had found in the portfolio in the tower.

"It all had something to do with a theory of gravity he was pursuing. He used her body, he used up her life, to serve his own disgusting intellectual greed. And there was probably an obscene pleasure for him in seeing her trussed up in that ghastly harness, performing for him like a puppet in the air."

"One day, while she was doing a glide, the wind suddenly dropped. The winds in the Border country are fickle. She fell and she died."

Callum stood up, his lovely face a rigid mask of pain. Instinctively, Suzanne stood too, reached across the table to touch his arm. His skin was cold. She was relieved that he did not pull away. Her urge was to walk around the table and hold him close. This task fell to Clara.

"Right," Jeremy said, after a moment's silence. "That's quite enough for now, I think. Children, how about one of the old games to break the spell. A complete change of pace is in order, I think. A tableau? Charades? A ballad?"

Suzanne was amazed to see both twins grow visibly calmer at Jeremy's suggestion. He is a magician with their moods, she thought. Then again: But, of course, he is their real father.

"A ballad," piped Clara. "How about Thomas? Jeremy, you make such a lovely road."

They were all three immediately on their feet, Jeremy a tall beacon in the centre, the twins on his either side. Jeremy began to recite:

True Thomas lay on Huntlie bank;
A ferlie he spied wi' his ee;
And there he saw a lady bright
Come riding down by the Eildon Tree.

Still reeling from the full force of the children's revelations, Suzanne found it difficult to concentrate on the words they recited with such intensity. It dawned on her that she was witnessing an apotropaic ritual: a theatrical performance that reinforced their bond to each other and made an imaginative world whose bounds repelled Murdo.

They were casting off Murdo's shadow. They were showing her one of the ways they had found to cleanse themselves of their father's corruption. She understood that they were extending her a great privilege. She remembered how Ada would burn sage or open the back door and breathe in the night air after she had dealt with a particularly demanding client. "Our survival depends on ritual, Suzanne, pure simple ritual, without the taint of blood. An homage to nature. Nothing else."

So Suzanne interpreted the children's performance for her and for themselves. Here was Callum become True Thomas and Clara the Queen of Elfland, trilling out her seductive invitation, twirling about on her slim feet: "Harp and carp, Thomas. Harp and carp and come along with me."

When Jeremy lay full-length on the floor, Suzanne was at first perplexed. But as Clara went on with the poem in her clear, sweet voice, Suzanne began to see that Jeremy was not now the narrator, but a road. In fact, three roads, one of which True Thomas must choose.

He lay to the right, his arms pressed tight to his sides, his expression pained, his whole body twitching. This was the narrow road of righteousness, set with thorns and briars. He lay to the left, like a drunk fallen on his back, arms akimbo, legs sprawled, a besotted grin on his face. This was the broad road, the path of wickedness. And for the middle road, the road to Elfland, which of course Thomas will choose, he lay between the twins, absolutely relaxed, his face smoothly beatific as a knight in effigy.

Clara could barely contain her mirth. Jeremy did indeed make a wondrous road, Suzanne thought. Then Jeremy was on his feet, once again the narrator, and too soon, it seemed to Suzanne, the ballad was at an end. Jeremy declaimed, an arm about either twin, his voice melancholic:

He hath gotten a coat of the even cloth,
And a pair of shoes of velvet green,
And till seven years were gone and past,
True Thomas on earth was never seen.

Suzanne applauded. Clara beamed. Callum's face flushed. Jeremy bowed.

"Oh, did you really like it?" Clara asked, as all three sat down again at the table. "We've never had an audience before, have we Jeremy?"

"No," he said. "Only invisible watchers."

"Yes," Clara said. "Shall we have a toast to Kirstie and Miranda."

"To Kirstie and Miranda, then," said Jeremy, raising his glass. As they all did, everyone at the table. Suzanne felt the heavy burden of the truth settle on her again. She knew she had painful days ahead, with the absorption of that truth and the making resolute of her will to confront Murdo. Her feeling for him was, at the moment, a burnt dead taste in her mouth.

Jeremy put his hand over hers and if she had the least doubt about the three's sincerity, it disappeared at that instant. "Will you be all right," he asked, "if we leave you for a while? I want to take the twins into Edinburgh to break the mood. But this all must be a terrible shock to you."

Both Callum and Clara were also watching her with concern. And so she smiled, as bravely as she knew how.

"You could take a walk to Thomas's stone," suggested Clara. "Couldn't she, Jeremy? And we'd likely be back by the time you returned. It's between Melrose and St. Boswells. The stone marks the spot where Thomas met the Queen of Elfland. I'll get the map to show you exactly where." And Clara ran off.

"I'll just get my jacket and wallet," Callum said to Jeremy. But before leaving the room, he came to Suzanne and put his lips to her forehead. "You must leave him," he said quietly.

When she and Jeremy were alone, Suzanne began to cry.

"We're so sorry you had to meet him," said Jeremy, stroking her hand. "But we're sure you have the strength to survive his machinations and poisonous nature."

"Oh, yes," she said. "Without doubt I have the strength."

"Because there's more, I'm afraid, some of which only Callum can tell you, if he is able. He was the worst wounded of the three of us; that is, Murdo hated him the most."

"But I must at least tell you this, in case Callum is unable." He stopped; then leant over to whisper in her ear.

"It was Murdo who blinded Callum's eye. He threw a hammer at him. Callum was ten at the time."

Jeremy sat back again, and without looking at her, poured Suzanne another drink.

"Thank you," she said. "But I believe I've had enough."

"Yes," he said with a wry smile. "I believe we all have."

Clara appeared with the map, Suzanne's destination already marked with an X.

"It's quite a tramp," said Jeremy. "A good twenty miles round-trip, I'd guess. You'd best take a sandwich and something to drink. And stout shoes, of course. You do have some?"

Suzanne nodded.

"Oh, Jeremy," Clara exclaimed. "You are such a thoughtful, lovable old thing."

Suzanne laughed. Good, she thought. I am still able to do that.

"We'll be back by seven, I expect," Jeremy said, as he and Clara left. "You're quite sure you're all right?"

"Yes." I have the armour of your kindness and your truthfulness to put on, she thought. And she set about studying the map, readying herself mentally for her march.

13

Thomas the Rhymer's Stone

A favourite story of Ada's was how Aeolus gave Odysseus the bag of winds to help speed the ship home. A fearsome gift, a leather pouch tied with a silver wire that bulged and throbbed as the confined winds fought for primacy and release. Aeolus instructed Odysseus to free only one wind at a time from the pouch as he had need of it to change course. Instead, Odysseus's men opened the bag, for they thought it contained wine. The resulting tempest drove the ship back to the palace of Aeolus, who refused Odysseus further help because he was obviously not favoured by the gods.

For Ada, the whole point of this tale was that live thing, the stopped-up pouch that warred within itself, a hundred tempests heaving inside a confine of skin. Her skin. After a particularly gruelling exorcism, plucking dark remembrances from her client as one might draw barbs from flesh, Ada would become for a while that wild, silently wailing receptacle. This was the supreme price she paid for her gift. She could not draw the venom out of another's soul without sucking it into herself. So until her own release came, Ada would roam the house, trembling, striking out at nothing visible (at least to Suzanne), her shoulders twitching as if to throw off the strictures of a winding sheet. Suzanne learned that no ministrations on her part could ease her mother's distress. "It will pass," Ada would say brusquely. After some hours, she would at last be released, restored to the full dimension of herself, the whining alien currents stilled and banished.

The deed of magic returns threefold to the doer. Intellectually, Suzanne grasped this concept well enough. Yet watching the excruciating agony her mother sometimes underwent to bring her clients succour, Suzanne thought the threefold recompense puny enough.

Now as Suzanne walked by sheer force of will toward Melrose, she felt she experienced that same invasion of voices not her own. "I am being squatted by devils," Ada had once cried out. Suzanne had not then been familiar with the term *squat*, and only later realized that her mother must have learned it from a British sailor. But the edge of terror had been unmistakable, a terror that had spread its contagion that day to Suzanne. For if any one virtue characterized Ada, it was fearlessness.

She had heard her mother cry out, as much in horror as in anguish, and through contagion, had felt her own self hollowed out. She was an empty gourd. First, there was a ghastly silence of nothingness and Suzanne knew she was in a world forsaken by every imaginable god. Then there was the sibilance, which she recognized immediately as demons hissing between their teeth. Here was the very taunt of madness, the flicking of serpents' tongues against her eardrums.

The devils Ada exorcized that day were so virulent, they had spilled over to Suzanne. And the hideous colonization of the self Suzanne then underwent was nothing to what her mother suffered.

"I am squatted by devils." Suzanne walked, much as her mother had walked. The erect spine. The long stride. The steady rhythm that gradually became consonant with an undercurrent of earth beneath her. As she went on, Suzanne felt the clamour of the disjunct voices begin to subside. If she just kept moving, she might be able to separate the fact from the misconception, the honesty from the hubris. Look on it as a magical task, she told herself. Like the sorting of seeds.

She did find it disturbing that all three of Murdo's children were apparently such accomplished actors. They switched moods, faces, guises as smoothly as any stage veteran. She had wholeheartedly believed Callum's poor little mad boy act. She had believed too, in his tears.

She stopped for a moment to take the map from her backpack. As soon as her body was still, the inner voices grew louder and more insistent.

She gave the map a cursory glance, and saw she had at least five miles to go. She decided to pluck one voice out of the clamour, to try to begin to examine them, strand by strand.

The loudest voice was also the most inarticulate. This was Murdo's; or rather, Murdo's pain, stopped up in his throat, pressing down on his shoulders, making itself visible in the dark pouched flesh under his eyes. This was the tragic note that had drawn her in the very first place, a note she believed was already transmuted into a full-bodied music that plumbed universes. And now she must decide if that tragic tone were something quite other: hollow and all too sickeningly familiar. A discordant self-pity, all tricked out in a noble disguise. How many millions of men have seduced women in just this way, with a melancholy stare, a mute cry that if she will only climb the steps of the gallows and cut the rope, he will not hang?

Who else was there?

There was Jeremy saying Murdo was a monster.

There was Callum weeping.

There was Jeremy insulting her, saying her life's work was an indulgent mental dress-up game for pampered women. (No, that voice did not carry with total conviction. He had been far more responsive to her subsequently.)

There was Clara describing her father as a gobbling whale, with an unbridled lust for control.

There was Gemma saying: Marriage is bad for women's health.

There was Callum babbling at her feet.

There was Gemma saying: Talk to the children.

There was Callum weeping.

There was Miranda wailing for her baby. Her breasts are sore. Her hips bear the impression of a cloth tape measure pulled tight. (This voice was not a new one. Suzanne realized to her shame that it had persistently tried to claim her attention but that she had pushed it away.)

There was Murdo's breath in her ear during love-making, so hot it made a small furnace in the cavity and then spread a fire along her flesh, so that she writhed under or above him. This miraculous fire that extinguished her own separateness.

Or was it simply lust, a superficial and ultimately meaningless accident of two bodies that met, fit, and shuddered in intensest pleasure? Had she fallen into the clutches of the Demon Lover, thereafter to be consigned to Hell?

She thought she might already be in Hell.

She heard Kirstie scream as she fell in her harness, the artificial wings collapsing about her body.

She heard Callum cry out as his left eye filled with blood.

Jeremy whispered: It was Murdo who blinded Callum.

Was that it? Or were there more voices in this seething hive that was herself? This self that walked toward Melrose to see a stone that the children's tableau had revealed as her goal. For after their horrendous narrative, she had badly needed an imposed task.

In times of trouble, walk, said Ada. And fix on a destination, no matter what. A certain lamppost that sends a snake of light into the harbour. A tree whose bark you can finger and ask to share in its deep vegetative peace. Walk. The body's movement through air, and your feet touching the earth, your will fixed on your destination. All this will help your mind to settle.

I am walking, thought Suzanne, toward a stone that marks the place a human male met the Queen of the Fairies. A goal no more ludicrous than any other because it is tied to my tentative trust in the children.

In their dramatic rendering of the ballad, she had seen the shimmering edges of the imaginative world they erected against their father. She supposed she had been privileged. We never had an audience before, Clara said.

Far ahead of her on the horizon, the softly rounded hills looked eerily insubstantial, as if made of a concentrated blue-grey mist. All around her the Borders weather worked its habitual transformative sorcery. A swift uprising of wind, a scud of thick cloud, and a verdant hill went dungeon dark. This might be the mouth of Hell, or a gloomy exterior door that promised bliss inside.

Suddenly, just ahead, she saw a buff-coloured tablet, unostentatious, unremarkable even, except for its graceful ogival form. She approached the stone, crouched down, and traced her finger along the carved letters. *Here Thomas of Ercildoune met the Queen of the Fairies and so began Scottish literature.* No irony here or sentimentality. Take it or leave it, the stone implied.

Suzanne sat on the ground, her back supported by the solid breadth of the tablet. For the moment, the cacophony of insistent voices had subsided. She ate the sandwich and apple she had packed in her knapsack, and drank all of the tea in the thermos.

She wanted to go on walking. Simply walk forever and avoid the mounting evidence of Murdo's cruelty.

Why have you done this stupid thing? She thought of Callum's young white throat, of the straw in his hair, of his fingers stroking her bare foot. She thought of how she had so much wanted to put her arm around him.

She tried not to think of Callum; not to picture his mismatched eyes: the peerless, lucent blue one and the dead, opaque one for which Murdo, her husband, was responsible.

She hated that *h* word. Why had she entertained it at all? The careful management of husbandry. The mathematical controls of Murdo. The wife measured, weighed, and separated from her child.

The wife caught up in a harness and cruel wings. The children drilled. The boy beaten. The boy blinded.

The boy blinded. Why would they lie to her? Unless there were an inheritance they were loath to share with their father's new wife. But this idea did strike her as totally absurd. They all three lived, apparently, stripped to the bone, and were, if anything, even less materialistic than either she or Gemma.

And what money could there be, with the house mouldering and in disrepair? A sad, antiquated lumbering place whose every stone was steeped in pain.

Sugar? Gemma had asked. Was the house purchased with the profits from slave labour? She must remember to ask the children.

Sugar? The word was a hideous taste in her mouth. She had the sickening thought that this was somehow mixed with the taste of Murdo's semen. She spat. She bent over with a spasm in her midriff, a jolt like a cattle prod. She felt suddenly horribly sick and quite irrationally afraid. She thought of Ada and the courage of women. There was a strange tingling at the back of her head. She no longer felt ill. Instead, she was oddly energized, consumed by a fierce, wild force that she struggled to bring to a focus. She began to walk more quickly, every footstep laid down with such purpose, its objective might be the preservation of her own life. She was an enviably strong woman, she told herself, a strong woman covering ground.

Then she realized that the world around her had changed, the light no longer yielding and fluid but tinselly and artificial. She looked up at the sun and saw it smothered in a kind of white gauze. Then it disappeared altogether. Murdo is responsible, she thought. Murdo, the gobbling whale, has swallowed down the sun. Or he came in his lion form and took it in his mouth, as a lion will eat his children.

She walked and was fearful in this alien place. She walked and thought of her mother. She was aware that something had gone terribly wrong with her perception. She wondered if she had eaten anything that was slightly off. The sandwich had been wholemeal bread and cheese. No mouldy rye. No argot. The tea only Earl Grey in a thermos she had found on a top shelf in the kitchen. The effects of the whisky she had shared with the children had surely long passed.

Then these rational thoughts all evaporated because she was moving through a landscape consisting of great slabs of plate glass. These glass slabs were mammoth. The height of Egyptian pyramids, she thought wildly. The glass was gummed or smeared so that it was often difficult to make out the road ahead. This must be what it is like to look out of Callum's dead eye, she thought. Or perhaps I am looking, now, out of Murdo's heart.

Murdo has eaten his children. He has swallowed down the sun.

Her heart lightened a little to hear a child singing from somewhere high in the branches of a tree. She turned round and round, seeking the child out, and was shocked when she spied him. He was a bird-child, some Bosch-like hybrid, a child above the waist for the most part, but below he had flexing legs and the curled claws of a bird. And the mouth that shaped the song had no soft lips; only a hard, yellow, pointed beak. His was a sweet song, but disturbing, even maddening, because it too was hybrid, an uncomfortable fusion of two species.

She feared she was going mad. She knew she must keep going, get back to the house, lie down and sleep. Then the familiar order of the visible world would be restored. I can do this, she told herself. It is only a question of going back the way I have come. Of reversing what I have done. Whatever I am undergoing is nothing to what millions of women have endured before me, and are enduring now.

It was her feet, rather than her eyes, that recognized the gravelled surface of the circular driveway. With relief, she saw the house, its buff stone, the tower with its gleaming slate cap, all reassuringly substantial. There was a broad-backed black animal that stood guard by the front door, as if waiting patiently for her return. A mastiff? A small trained bear? Why had she never seen it before? The animal craned its neck toward her as she came up to it, obviously watching out for her. She stroked its shiny flanks as she went by and stumbled into the house.

Once she was inside, a piercing wind circled the house, although only seconds before the air had been sullenly still. She heard the heavy rain hurling itself against the winds. She could not understand why her own cheeks stung with this wind and rain.

I must find a book, she thought. The book I was reading yesterday evening. I will lie down on my bed and read, and in that familiar habit, I will find sleep. My arm will grow numb and my hand will drop and the open book will fold gently over my face.

Thinking she had left the book there, she went into the dining room. She could not at first comprehend the shadowy shape on the floor. As she came closer, she saw that it was Murdo, lying face down, a dagger driven up to the hilt into his neck. She froze. Or time froze. She was uncertain which. She wished this terrible deed undone. She wondered if she might have committed the murder or if it was the children's doing. She tried to move her feet, to go to the telephone. I must get an ambulance, she thought. He might still be alive.

She found she could not move. She just stood staring at the handle of the dagger. It looked like some frightful excrescence he had grown overnight, like a beak or an antler. The knife handle did in fact appear to be made of horn, a substance darkly obdurate, and with a natural whorl, whose curves the maker had followed in shaping it for the hand's grip. Embedded in the hilt was a cairngorm. The dagger was apparently a classical Scottish dirk, possibly centuries old. She wanted to take the blade out of Murdo's neck, wipe off the blood, slit time apart, and then go back to where they had been.

She got her wish. She actually heard the membrane of time being ripped apart. Then she realized this sound was in fact the red velvet curtain opening, swishing and swaying as someone tugged on the pulley. And there they stood. Jeremy in the middle as ever, flanked by Callum and Clara, all three with clean, prim faces, their hands clasped neatly in front. They looked at her. They looked at the dead body of Murdo. They nodded and smiled. And in unison, they began to clap.

The room exploded then into shards of light. The red of blood. The yellow of egg yolk. The black of putrid water. The last thing Suzanne remembered was a splinter of blue light piercing her eye. And the flood of understanding that accompanied the pain.

Now I am blinded too. Now I will forever be bound to Callum.

14

Callum

Callum's eye socket was throbbing. He was upset, "in a state," Clara had said, before setting him the task of a hill run. They had always said "hill run" when they were children, and he had laughed when she used the phrase, felt briefly and fadingly exuberant, as if he could indeed launch himself back to innocence simply by jogging up the smooth flank of a Border hill.

To please Clara, he had complied. And now he sat on a rocky outcrop of a sturdy enough hill, surveying the gently undulating vista beneath. Too gentle for his taste, but pleasing, of course, with its green humps set off by patches of yellow broom and rust-red bracken. The pull of this Borders country had subsided for him forever, once he had seen and tasted the wildness of the North. When he first saw the northwest of Scotland, through the windows of the little steam train chugging its way from Glasgow to Oban, he had been awestruck, even a little frightened. He simply had not known that his country, so very small when you looked at it on a map, contained such rugged vastness. A godly vastness. The naked mountains had seemed to press in, threatening to engulf the tiny train on all sides. Yet the more he looked, the more he loved them. They called to something fiercely vital in his blood, that wild, impulsive part of himself that would not be quelled. Nor would he ever wish it so. For above all, it was his impulsiveness that distinguished him from Murdo.

Murdo hated the North. "A raw, uncivilized place," he used to say, whenever Kirstie wanted to go home to Mull. And so she had gone alone, taking him and Clara. That first time on the train, once his fear settled, he had wanted to pierce the glass of the window, yield himself up to the surging power of the place. Later, as a teenager, he had gone with a girlfriend to Glencoe. There he had trembled and wept. The girl was initially sympathetic. She thought he was over-tired or had a cold. Then she had chided him and laughed at him. He had trouble with girls, and even now, with young women his own age. His most successful love affairs were always with older women. They had a breadth of wisdom that did not intrude. They did not think him either feckless or mad.

He had intended by now to be well away from these Border hills. He had wanted to take the bike up the Applecross Peninsula, that tortuous ascent to a height from which you could see Skye, lying in the water like a dark blue beast. And where the barren ground was covered with cairns, lovingly laid by God knows how many thousands of hands. He thought of these cairns as revenants. They were all spirits who had loved that place and come back. You could hear them whispering when you stood there.

Even in a car, the zigzag drive to the top was perilous. With each inch forward, you feared you would fall off the narrow, twisting road. On the bike it would be wondrous, his body and the Triumph pitching themselves forward against gravity. Against fear. Against the very edge of life. Or of death.

But the "incident" as Jeremy termed it, had sent his plans haywire. Jeremy and Clara had tried to absolve him of blame. But when they found her and he spotted the thermos poking out of her knapsack, he knew right away what had happened. He was responsible, if only indirectly. He was dreadfully sorry if her experience had been frightful.

Clara was with her now. They had carried her to bed, he and Jeremy and Clara, and laid cooling cloths on her forehead. Her pulse was good although she was a little drained looking and quite limp. Her head would probably ache when she woke. Her mouth would be dry. They could easily right that. But he wanted to be there when she woke up. He must explain what had happened and how it was his fault, really.

So his trip to Applecross must be delayed another day. Time was tight, uncomfortably so. He sensed Murdo's approach like a smothering shadow. Clara had taken the call. Two days, the pater announced. He would return in two days. Callum could not bear the idea of encountering him. The sight of that smug leonine countenance made him physically ill. And those thick shoulders encased in musty tweed. Retch.

Through the distant treetops, he thought he could make out the dull gleam of the slate that topped the house's round tower. He had swung from its conical peak at least twice he could remember. Looping the lasso over the roof tip had been the difficult part. He had had to crouch on a narrow, crumbling window ledge, over a drop that induced a rush of vertigo he could feel still in the soles of his feet. Once the loop was secure, he had swung out on the rope, making himself a human pendulum, working against the force of gravity that Murdo had made his particular intellectual province.

They had all three done it in their own way, swung out against the horrendous sucking gravity that was Murdo. Jeremy took more real risks than he or Clara. They both worried about him constantly, as Jeremy deliberately put his body and mind under threat, reporting on ethnic wars, displaced persons' camps, child prostitution rings, child slave labour. He admired Jeremy immensely, and it hurt him to see

his brother contort himself in ethical knots, berating himself
because, in a sense, he made a living from others' pain. Jeremy
subjected every word he wrote and spoke, his every action,
to the most rigorous moral scrutiny. Whereas Murdo simply
grabbed and ate and choked off and forced and beat and lay
stinking in his own Slough of Despond.

Clara had escaped the paternal force field by the very
lightness of her feet and her shape-shifting on stage. She
could make you laugh or cry in the same minute. She could
change in a second from demure nun to imp to chimp to
chicken to fairy. Clara was his solace, the one who had always
understood his secret language.

For himself, he had sometimes plunged too far in his
effort to differentiate himself from the wretched pater. And
the most terrible time was when he was obsessed about the
genes he must have inherited from Murdo. The anxiety had
clawed like a rat at his brain. What if – despite his own
blessed waywardness and all he must have inherited from
Kirstie – what if those genes of Murdo's suddenly asserted
themselves and he became what he most wished not to
become. So for a time, he had given himself all too willingly
to drugs. Coke, Ecstasy, even heroin for a while. Here was a
risk-taking he did not care to repeat. That had been his most
precipitous drop. For a time, his secret language was all he
was able to speak, if he spoke at all. Like the boy who cried
wolf, he had played with that strange language of his own
making and it had taken him over.

The people of the streets had saved him. Their compassion and dignity had borne him up, but of course he had
been lucky in those he met. In a sense, he had always been
lucky. He tried to give back what he had been given, volun-
teering with an organization that worked for the homeless.
After a time he got paid; not a lot, but enough to live, and he
still had some of the money he and Clara had inherited from
Kirstie. Which was what had bought the bike.

It was his idea that the organization solicit donations of fur coats to help the street people survive the winter. For many of the homeless hated the confinement of government-run shelters. They preferred the freedom, the integrity of their makeshift bedrooms set up on the pavement: a cardboard canopy, a treasure trove of polyethylene bags, an ancient blanket whose odours reassured them they were home. The fur coat owners were only too willing to liberate themselves of guilt garments. Who, after all, wants to be spat on in the street and called an animal murderer? But to satisfy all parties – particularly the anti-trapping brigade – the coats had to be defaced. Before leaving London, Callum had therefore put many hours into ripping seams and sleeves from capes and cloaks and full-length manteaus of seal and lynx and mink. Then he had taken a spray can of paint (guaranteed ozone-friendly) and played noughts and crosses on the glistening fur.

There were times, he thought, when the indulgences of the well-off could be very profitably exploited.

He had taken up photography for just that reason, building an archive of documentary evidence to prod the conscience of the rich. Rather than photograph the people of the streets themselves, he had focused on their pavement beds – "bashes" they called them. Always, he had asked, and generally been given, the owner's permission. When he developed these photos, he was floored by their mute eloquence. A box, a block of Styrofoam, a Harrod's shopping bag, a shredded red comforter. Juxtaposed, these objects pleaded more articulately than could words. No – "pleaded" was of course the wrong word, suggesting debasement, grovelling. Spoke, then. By some miracle, the photographs spoke, far more succinctly and lucidly than his own tongue could ever manage.

He sometimes wondered if those early years of fractured babble, the nonsense language he had cultivated in part to evade and infuriate his father, had spoiled him for speech for life. Why else did he so often find himself struck dumb by what he saw? Sometimes with a terrible raw rage, sometimes in simple amazement at human tenacity, the sheer will required to make a home out of garbage, to trundle one's belongings through the street in a hijacked shopping cart. The underclass (as the newspapers called the dispossessed) was increasing all the time, and getting younger too. And unfortunately, the world seemed full of evil men, like his father, who had no compunction about preying on young bodies. This made him sick and afraid because he did not know how to help other than in doing what he did.

Not even Jeremy had short-term answers. Jeremy had seen his photographs and arranged a meeting with the owner of a Cork Street gallery. In September, there was to be an exhibition of *The Bashes* by Callum Napier. While he was pleased, he was also uneasy. Any publicity of the plight of the homeless is good, said Jeremy. Yet it was also from Jeremy that he had learned the habit of self-scrutiny, that trawling of the heart to uncover motives suspicious or unworthy. It bothered him immensely that he might profit, even meagrely, from someone else's pain.

They all practised self-scrutiny, he and Jeremy and Clara. In this way, they ensured that they belonged to a totally different class of being than Murdo.

Jeremy was the adept and unflinching self-examiner. Callum thought he would never be able to approximate his brother's standards. There were aspects of himself so repulsive he could face them only with the greatest difficulty. His dreams of parricide, for example. They still at times shook him awake at night. He would be drenched in sweat, doubled over with vile stomach cramps, much as he had been when he came off heroin. Always the same dream. He stood over his father's dead body, which lay face down, with a dagger driven in its back. And he, Callum, looked down with his fist still clenched, the muscles of his right arm taut as wire.

When he woke from these dreams, the fingers of his right hand would be knotted and painful.

It might so easily have actually happened, he realized. Were it not for Jeremy and Clara and old Nanny and a chain of fortunate circumstance he could only attribute to inexplicable luck. For God knows, he had wished Murdo dead often enough.

And now there was this new element he must face when he trawled through his own sore heart. This totally unexpected desire for his father's third wife. He had agonized over his feelings since he first saw her come into the outbuilding, looking like a proud and stunning Gypsy woman. This was all so terribly mythic, Oedipal almost, and he had racked himself with brutal questioning. Was he attracted to Suzanne because stealing her away would be tantamount to killing Murdo? Did he want her simply as a means to perpetrate an act of vengeance?

He thought not. He truly thought not. His first sight of her had indeed struck him dumb. The old language was back. He was babbling and at her feet. And he was there because that was exactly where he wanted to be. When he had stoked her bare foot. Well, for the moment, he did not dare think about it.

Yet he must. Almost the instant he saw her, he wanted to photograph her. From the waist up, in a black silk shawl, with a long fringe of dangling tassels. That would be all she would wear, so that the inner rounds of her breasts showed beneath the fall of black silk. And then another portrait of her, full-length, the shawl floating on her shoulders, the rest of her gloriously naked. It was dusk and she stood beside a fire on a shoreline by the sea. The flames danced in obeisance to her beauty. The mountains around her were a dark purple. He knew this place. He knew it was in the North. He thought perhaps it was in the Hebrides. He knew the place and he knew her.

He had grown hard with desire, picturing himself going up to her and kneeling down and putting his arms about her hips and his face…

This was most perilous ground, he knew. More perilous than that first time he had put the needle in his vein and sunk into the deep blanketing warmth that preceded the nod into bliss. More perilous than walking a ridgepole, five storeys up, daring gravity to take you down and silence your heart forever.

But whatever happened, they had all three agreed. They must do what they could to encourage her to leave Murdo.

He must somehow spirit her away. What a wonderful verb, he thought. And how fitting in this case. His spirit would liberate hers from the bone crusher, the heart eater, the wretched smothering cloud that was his father.

He had a plan. And when she woke he would tell her everything.

15

Walking the Ridgepole

She dreamt of a full lip pressed between her own, as lusciously plump as a peach. She dreamt of lovemaking so fine, so drawn out, that it verged on being unbearable. She dreamt that she was Thomas the Rhymer, gone underground in a suit of green silk. She dreamt she was the Queen of Fairyland, riding Thomas to a fine point of ecstasy. Then she was the two-in-one, that mystical state her girlhood had yearned for.

Then she had an anvil in her head and a throat parched and sore and she thought that perhaps she had drunk too much wine. Or mead. What exactly had she drunk in that place underground?

When she opened her eyes, there were two blond angels leaning over her, their faces watchful and concerned. Had she died then?

It was Clara who spoke first: "Oh, are you all right? We've brought you some Paracetamol and a pitcher of water."

Suzanne recognized the voice but could not immediately place it. The person who spoke belonged to some long-ago past and the utterance came through a tunnel in time. Then Clara made one of her characteristic skipping motions up to the bed. And so Suzanne emerged into the present. Here were the delightful, bubbling Clara and the strange and beauteous Callum. And there had been Jeremy too. And all three had told her tales of Murdo's behaviour…

The anvil in her head began to rock and press its edges into the most tender parts of her brain. She groaned aloud.

"Oh God," said Callum. "Oh my God, I am so sorry. It's my fault. It's all my fault."

"Shut up, Callum." Clara hissed. "Suzanne, take this Paracetamol, please. It will help, I'm sure."

Suzanne swallowed the pills with a little water. Breathe deeply, Suzanne. Visualize an opening in the pain. What has been done can be undone. Visualize an opening. A milk-white dawn is pushing back the night.

She sat up, and Clara helped prop the pillows behind her head.

"Shall I heat you up a little chicken broth, Suzanne?"

Suzanne nodded. Then suddenly she remembered. The body with the dagger in its neck, a piece of horn where a horn should not be. A whipcord of panic seized her body: "Murdo?" she gasped. "Where is Murdo?"

"He'll be here," Clara responded. "Tomorrow."

A dream then, thought Suzanne. Only a dream.

"Ugh!" said Callum.

"Do shut up, Callum. Stay with Suzanne while I make the soup. And don't upset her."

He put on such a hangdog expression that Suzanne almost laughed.

As soon as Clara was out the door, he came and sat on the edge of the bed.

"Is this all right?" he asked, and gingerly, he took her hand in his own.

"Yes." In fact, his proximity was helping. She felt her headache lift as he stroked the back of her hand.

"I must have had a hallucination," she told him. "I saw Murdo dead on the floor of the dining hall with a dagger protruding from his back."

"My God," Callum said softly. "You had my dream."

"It's my fault, you see," he went on. "There was powdered opium in that thermos. I'd forgotten I put it there a couple of summers ago. Or maybe I didn't really forget. Maybe unconsciously I wanted the wretched pater to take it. Any visions he had would certainly be of the tormenting variety. Oh, I don't know." His face twisted in anguish. "I am so sorry it was you who found the stupid thermos. I'm so terribly sorry. Was it very awful for you?"

Without thinking what she did, Suzanne caressed his cheek. "It's all right. It's over now," she reassured him. "I'm really quite resilient, you know."

She saw that he was crying. And so it seemed wholly fitting when he lay his head between her breasts and she began to stroke his hair. "It's really all right, Callum." She could feel the patch of wetness spreading on her T-shirt.

He lifted his head. "It's not just the opium thing," he said. "It's everything. It's dredging up the memories, but we had to do that for your sake. And it's the horrible thought of you with him and the damage he might do to you."

She went on stroking his hair, just as she wanted to do when he knelt before her in the outbuilding. "I can look after myself, you know."

And then there it was, even as it had been in the dream before she woke into the presence of the angels. Lips that touched hers with the softness and scent of grapes. Then his full bottom lip pressed deep between her own. And under the thin sheet that covered her, her whole body blazed with a desire to feel his nakedness against her, to have him inside her. Sweet Mother, she thought, I am bewitched. And then: But of course I am. I am my mother's daughter.

Yet she had the sense to push him firmly away. "Callum," she said firmly. "This is all rather too complicated."

He sat back, immediately complying. His huge eyes were still wet. The artificial one looked red-rimmed and sore.

Murdo did that, she thought. Murdo did that. Her stomach knotted.

"Clara is coming," Callum said. They both heard the old stair creak as Clara made her way up to the bedroom.

"Look," he said. "It's a lovely day. Why don't we take a walk this afternoon?"

She started to speak. Callum put his finger to his lips.

"Nothing will happen, I promise. The fresh air will help you. Believe me, I know about curing opium hangovers. And there's more I absolutely must tell you. Will you?"

Callum left as Clara came in. Suzanne watched him go and he turned to look at her just before he went out the door. The tenderness of his regard confirmed all that she feared. He believes he is in love with me. And what is worse, I believe I could only too easily reciprocate. Have I gone quite mad?

She looked up to find Clara watching her intently.

"Yes," Clara said, setting the tray with the bowl of soup on the bedside table. "I know. He told me."

"The question is," Clara continued. "Will it make matters better or worse?"

Suzanne ate her soup. For the moment, there was nothing more to be said.

What mysteries families are, thought Suzanne.

They walked. Callum had not tried to touch her. She had not taken his hand. He walked ahead of her and kept silent. She knew without his telling her that they were making their way to the outbuilding with its flowering roof.

"Let's climb up to the loft," he said, once they were inside and had lit the old lamp.

She followed him up the ladder, where she settled on a thicket of straw. Callum sat a few feet away, his elbows propped on his knees. He rubbed his eyes and began.

"I'll start with this, shall I?" He put his index finger to the lid of his blind eye. "Clara said Jeremy told you. But I know if you ask Murdo about it, he'll lie. He'll tell you it was an accident at school or some such bullshit. But he did throw the hammer at me, and the worst thing was, I gave him no provocation."

"I was ten years old. He'd always hated me, as long as I could remember. Probably because Grandmamma (that was his mother) and Kirstie both doted on me. Or so he said. He was quite vicious when it came to corporal punishment, although thank God, he never touched Clara. I was afraid of him and I hated him. When he was at home, I used to come up here to hide."

"But," he sighed deeply. "Back to the day with the hammer. I went into the playroom. I didn't know he was there, obviously. He never went in there. He took so little interest in anything we did. Except for school results and the drills and observing the most rigid forms of politeness with our elders. I scored rather badly in all these areas. At any rate, I went in and there he was, waiting for me in the playroom. It frightened the life out of me."

"I swear to you that I said or did nothing to make him do it. I just came in and there he was with the hammer in his hand. And why? He is certainly no handyman. He'd think household repairs beneath him. One pays the lower orders to do such things. I was standing at the door and he was across the room and I saw this dark object flying at me and then there was just the most awful pain."

"So, that's it, really. That's the way it happened. Nanny told me long afterwards that Murdo got quite drunk that night after they took me to the Infirmary in Edinburgh. Kirstie was in a state, of course. He told her I'd lunged at him like a mad thing, before he could put the hammer down and that I'd rammed my face right into the clawed end. She must have believed him. I stopped talking for quite a while after

that so I never told her. But I did tell Clara. I always spoke to
Clara. She can understand my babble talk, you see."

"Right?" he said. "Are you still with me?"

"Yes." And he can take that however he wishes, she
thought. The pictures in her mind were hellish. To do such a
thing to a child. But what if Callum were wrong? What if he
had reconstructed the incident out of his hatred? Not that he
was lying. Only that he had recast what happened to suit his
image of the ogre parent. Was it possible?

He took a deep breath and stared out into the dusky vac-
uum below.

"The next thing I'll tell you happened about two years
after Kirstie's death. So I must have been thirteen." He
stopped again. Suzanne yearned to be nearer him. But
thought better of it.

"He took pictures of her when she did her glides. He
would push her to repeat the arc, time after time. She was
tired, you know. She had us; we were a handful. I didn't eat
glass then, though. All that came later. But the worst was…
the worst."

He had closed his eyes. She saw his shoulders tremble.
"The worst was that he photographed her after she had
fallen. Her mouth gaping at one side, blood running there
and from her eyes. And a slackness about her whole body, a
kind of softness, as you'd see in a newborn baby. Except with
her, it was because all her bones were broken."

He was speaking to her still with his eyes shut tight, and
he put out his hand to her blindly. She took it; he grasped hers
so firmly, she could feel his pulse beating through her skin.

"How did you come to see this photograph?" she asked
him, phrasing the question as gently and quietly as she could,
conscious of the shock the image of his dead mother still
posed for him.

"The pater showed me." Callum's customary insouciance
seemed to have returned. He opened his huge eyes, jerked

his chin upwards. Or was this simply the face of defiance he must put on whenever Murdo was mentioned?

"Murdo?" Of course, she did not want to believe it. There could be no justification whatever for showing a child a photograph of his mother, dead and broken. Such an act was pure sadism.

"Yes," he said, and the tremble again in his shoulders told her it was true.

"But why…?" She was glad that he still held her hand.

"Why?" he repeated. "Pater's obscene version of punishment, I suppose." He pushed his free hand through the mass of springing curls. "I'd been suspended from boarding school. I'd been caught walking the ridgepole. Except that it was the third time I'd been caught. And I was wearing only the school blazer, you see. Nothing else on at all. One gets rather a big erection walking ridgepoles five floors up."

He laughed and Suzanne began to see how necessary, how joyful, these acts of rebellion had been. Every caper, every scrape, had been a sweet loosening of Murdo's control.

"The school was afraid of being sued, I suppose, lest I fall. And probably the fact I was naked under the blazer shocked the headmaster's wife. She was quite proper, you see. Unlike matron, who was unshockable after years and years of exposure to her boys."

"So, I got sent home. I was summoned into pater's presence. He beat me on the buttocks till I bled. He had a special cane for discipline, you know. I presume," he opened his good eye slyly, "that he never used it on you."

"Callum!" She had let go of his hand at this last remark, but now he sought the close grip of her fingers again.

"Sorry," he said. "It's just that I wanted to avoid, put off, getting to the photo… Anyway," he took a deep breath. "Once I had my pants done up, standing before him, head bowed – that was the required post-discipline stance, eyes to the floor, compliant. If I didn't assume that position, that guilty expression, he would use the cane on my face. I only risked that once. It's possible to endure an awful lot of stripes on the buttocks."

"Then, Murdo said, 'Come here boy, I've something to show you.' He had the photos in an envelope in his desk drawer."

"And he made me look at them. He made me…"

Callum wept. Suzanne had never seen a sight more piteous.

She put her around about him.

When he recovered himself, they both climbed a little shakily down the ladder and out into the light of day.

He took her hand. "Now you know it all," he said.

"Clara and I will both be off today," he added.

Hearing this, Suzanne felt bereft.

"I'll take her into Edinburgh to catch her train" he continued. "But I'll be staying with some friends in Innerliethen for a couple of days. I'll give you the phone number there. If you want out or you want help, just call. I'll only be half an hour away on the bike. Pack a small bag in case you do want to come with me. Please say you will. We are all of us so afraid for you."

"Yes," she said. "It's very kind of you." And I may well need a speedy exit, she thought. And yes, I do not want this to be the last time I see Callum, whatever that may mean.

He looked extremely relieved. Then he grinned, and did a little impromptu jig.

"I could take you to the most wonderful place," he announced. "A place that would purify you of any contact you've had with him. Have you seen the Highlands?"

"No. But Callum, I must speak with Murdo. I must hear what he has to say. I did marry him." She stopped. The sentence made a nasty taste in her mouth. Yet she was the one who had done the deed.

"I know. I know," he cried out. "And it's truly horrible that you did."

She watched the twins drive off on the bike. Her sense of loss was acute, like bidding goodbye to her own innocence.

Clara had kissed her and given her her post office address in York. And a message from Jeremy: "He says he is so sorry he was rude to you and that you must call him when you're back in London. And that he will definitely read one of your books."

"And he will, you know." She gave one of her emphatic little nods.

How very exquisite they are, thought Suzanne as she went back into the house to face her own dread.

And isn't it odd that I see nothing of Murdo in any of them?

16

A Letter to Ada

Dear Ada:
The lights have just gone out. A summer storm has torn out of the North Sea. Rain pummels the window. In the light of the candle flame, the pane of glass is a waterfall. The glass has melted. Nothing is as it seemed.

The night and the wind and the rain press at the window. These were the first gods, the weather gods, as you told me so long ago. The wind batters at the glass and the stone walls. If I were mad, I might run outside to be drenched by that rain, thrown to my knees by the wind.

As it is, I will sit here in the dining hall, where so much has lately been revealed, writing this letter to you. The movement of the pen across the page helps bridle my restlessness. The flicker of the candle flame is a silent tongue. It reassures me, with its endless thirst for new form. When I am finished, I will feed this letter to the flame.

Ada, I think now I have made a grave error of judgement. The grave is where he sent two trusting women, according to his children. I am numb still at what they have seen fit to tell me.

I thought he was other than he is. How many women have made this same lament? We could forge a chain of our

cries that would reach back to the beginning of time. I am
one of the very fortunate ones. I am free to leave and he has
as yet done me no real damage. Except of course, this continuing nausea and yes, I must confess it, an abiding hurt
pride.

Whatever happens, I will not be seduced by the idea I
can redeem him. I will not make his salvation my life's work.
I know far too many women who have squandered their talents in this way.

Yet I must also consider whether my condemnation of
Murdo is too hasty. Is the evidence against him merely cir-
cumstantial? I have no doubt he would be found innocent in
a court of law, except perhaps, for his brutal treatment of
Callum.

It comes down again, as so often, to a question of belief.
I believe the children when they speak of what he has done.
The pain in their eyes, and in the rigid set of their bodies, is
unmistakable. If I had any doubts, Callum banished them. I
think of him as my angel of deliverance. But like all angels, he
poses great risks. His wings are, I think, made of fire. I cannot
dwell on thoughts of Callum now. This is not the time.

Let me return to my grievous error. How did I go this
wrong? I am most guilty, I think, of the sin of projection. I
projected my own girlish desires on to a man of clay. I
wanted the cataclysmic, burgeoning passion that would lead
to the sacred marriage. In Murdo I chose, as we so often do,
the exact opposite of what I wished.

The fault is mine. I was the one who read into his silence
the exalted workings of a deep soul. I was the one who saw
his suffering as rendering him thoughtfully compassionate. In
fact, all these things appear true of Jeremy. Murdo, on the other
hand, is apparently callous, wickedly selfish, a pathetic egotist.

The sexual relation was powerful. Indubitably. But there
too, I read far more into it than was on offer. I wonder now
if Murdo is simply superbly practised. He is after all, over

sixty. He has had plentiful time to learn what gives women pleasure.

I do not think I could bear the proximity of his flesh ever again.

I did leap into this marriage. Gemma warned me. Other women friends warned me.

I think I felt weighed upon by dogma. I have become disenchanted with my own discipline. Feminist study has become a commodity – more, an industry – with factions at each other's throats. So it has become "divide and conquer." We lose sight of what matters most in this war of books and theory. We are in danger of becoming our own enemies.

There is a chilling truth in what Jeremy says. Chilling but fortifying. My books are just pretty picture stories in a sense. Pictures of aspects of the female psyche. The Virgin. The Sensual Woman, so often condemned as the Whore. I saw my books as reclamations of our integrity. Little rafts of hope to bear us up in a world that belittles and maligns us. In the "free" western world, our conditioning is so subtle, so pervasive, that often we are unaware of it. Of course, I am highly sensitized to see misogyny, male condescension, and arrogance where others are blind to them. Some would say I am overly sensitized.

I have learned to mistrust men who protest how much they "respect" women. Most often, they protest too much. They are in fact the ones most certain of their superiority as a sex.

What are the roots of misogyny, Ada? This is the abiding question that plagues me night and day. Is it the fact that men cannot control our thoughts? For we do, I believe, perceive and think far differently than they do. Through association and connections, women seem to weave an invisible web that may well be what sustains the physical and spiritual worlds. Or is the root of misogyny because we can produce life, and men cannot? Or cannot, fortunately, to this point.

Then there are the wrong-headed patriarchal notions that persist over millennia, that hang in the air like vile spore. Aristotle's notion that woman is an inferior version of man. Or the grimly punitive tale of Eve, whose folly brought sin into the world.

I am struck hard by the foul language of the two priests who wrote the *Malleus Malificarum*. Yet here is the justification for the torture and murder of millions of women over three centuries. The numbers are naturally enough in dispute. It is said that we feminists exaggerate; that there was not enough wood in Europe to lay the pyres to burn that many women. This seems to me a facile argument. Where hatred is rife, men will always find a way to kill the object of their hatred. Hanging, for example. James I, the son of Mary Queen of Scots, hung more witches than any other British monarch.

"What else is woman but a foe to friendship, an inescapable punishment, a necessary evil, an evil of nature?" This from the *Malleus*, rightly called "The Hammer of the Witches." It seems to me that these ideas hammer still at all women.

As a result of my marriage, I find myself now in a country where the "witch craze" was particularly cruel and protracted. Women in Scotland were burned as witches as late as the 1750s. And that same James I (then James VI of Scotland) was obsessed with hunting out and persecuting women thought to be possessed by the foul fiend. His treatise "On Demonology" contains a rationalization of torture that many governments still endorse: "Loath are they to confess without torture which witnesseth their guiltiness."

Thus we have: one Agnes Simpson, an elderly woman of good education, who was examined by the king himself and then stripped and shaved to make it easier for her tormentors to seek out the devil's mark. She was shackled to a wall, with the prongs of the witch's bridle lacerating her cheeks.

An elderly woman of good education. She was kept without sleep. Naturally, she confessed.

I find I cannot go on with this book I had begun. In part, I wanted to do it for you. But I am appalled and stunned by the sadism and suffering my research has uncovered. My anger threatens to overcome me so that I would be in danger of writing polemic.

I see the witch burnings now as institutionalized mass murder. Not the blip, the negligible aberration in European history that we were taught in school. This socially sanctioned abuse and murder of women persists. In Pakistan, married women are hacked to death if they are so much as seen in the company of a man other than their husbands. Impoverished women in India kill their own female babies because it is preferable to have a son, because a girl child will some day require a dowry. And how can that poor mother and her husband ever afford a dowry? And so she smashes her own baby's head against the wall, or feeds her dry grains of rice so that she chokes to death.

Every day my friend Gemma comforts women who have been humiliated, beaten, left for dead. To blame poverty or alcoholism is too glib. The roots go far deeper. The yin has been torn away from the yang. It is as simple and as deadly as that, and it has been true for millennia. As I grow older, I find this fact no easier to confront.

I am not yet able to write the book I must write. I am uncertain how to make myself able. You were right. Anger is a potent demon. If I could learn to leash this rage and grief, I might be equal to the undertaking.

But my own balance is quite thrown off. For now I am weeping again. And to my shame, I am crying in part for myself. And for Miranda and Kirstie and for Callum.

Yet what if I am wrong? What if the children are wrong? If they misread or grossly misinterpreted what happened because Murdo was an excessively stern and unloving father?

What do I know of fathers? Or of how a gulf between a father and his children might spawn hatred, and that hatred colour his every word and deed?

What if I am condemning Murdo out of hand? Then I too would be guilty of the witch hunt. Or warlock hunt. Seek out the wicked man. You have no farther to look than your own bed.

And yes, I have the tools of torture. Were I to tell him that I have kissed his son on the mouth, held his head between my breasts, he would suffer terribly.

Of course, I will not tell him. I could not do that.

I cannot think of Callum now.

So I will wait until Murdo comes. And I will confront him finally with what the children have told me.

His silence must yield. I will listen and I will make my decision.

His silence must yield. If it does not, he will have made my decision for me.

I will burn this letter to you now, Ada, in the candle flame that is like a yellow pennant fluttering.

17

Clarity Must Come

Suzanne rose at six, bathed, and put on jeans and a long, loose shirt of cadmium blue. On the back of a chair, she laid out a warm sweater and her jean jacket. The night before she had packed her knapsack with a complete change of clothes, a second sweater, a notebook and several pens. Inside the notebook she tucked her favourite photograph of Ada, standing in their backyard in Halifax, laughing into the sun.

She was ready for flight, if flight it must be. In her back pocket, she had the slip of paper with the phone number Callum had given her. A talisman, she thought. Odd that it should consist of digits, when numbers were apparently one of Murdo's means for tormenting Callum. "Everything is number," Murdo had once told her. She had read into that statement his intuition of the mystery of the cosmos, a theurgy even. Instead, he had perhaps meant simply that. Nothing Pythagorean, nothing that alluded to the music of the spheres. Just numbers. Everything terminated where the equation ended.

She pulled back the curtain and opened the window. Outside, the early morning light was peerless. Everything shone – the flanks of the far-off hills, tree bark and greensward – as if mesmerized by its own essence. When she and Ada walked by the harbour, the light reflected off the sea was sometimes a great wheel, edged with silver. "We love light because we are light," said Ada. "Let it fill your head and your spine. Drink it down."

She realized she was standing at the window as her mother used to stand, her hands planted firmly on her hips. That was Ada at the window, watching the world.

I am standing at the window, Suzanne thought, just as my mother used to stand.

Yet here is an essential difference. Ada never married. I did not know my father. He died, she said. He was dark, and of course, handsome. Of Romany extraction. That was all I ever knew.

He died and I did not miss what I did not know. We were enough. Mother and daughter.

Ada never married. It was I who married.

Suzanne heard a car door slam. The sound emptied her head of every thought but one: Now it begins.

She went to the top of the stair and looked down. He stood in the open doorway, as if hesitating, uncertain whether to enter his own home. His briefcase and travelling bag were propped at his feet.

Murdo kept his face turned away from her as she came slowly down the stairs. He seemed not to hear her, to be frozen in thought. The slab of outdoor light behind him was pitiless. She saw every seam of his face, the tight puckering of dark flesh beneath his eyes. Never had he looked so old to her, or indeed, so fragile. A stoop in his shoulders she had not registered before diminished his stature. He is an aging lion, she thought. Or did she see him differently now because she no longer looked at him through the eyes of unsullied love?

As she came up closer to him, she felt a wash of emotion she could not immediately identify. Compassion? Then it struck her it was simply sorrow. A grieving for him and his alienation from his children. And a grieving for what else?

She fought back the urge to touch him. He looked small and ailing, but she recognized this might well be Gemma's man nailed to the cross. It is a trick, she thought. A ploy with nails and wood and a suffering face.

"'Murdo," she said. "We must talk."

Her voice apparently electrified him. His shoulders squared. His eyes cleared.

"The gang of three have been working their propaganda, have they? I suppose I ought not to have left you alone with them. But I did think you would have the sense to see through their charades... Yes, yes. By all means, let us talk. I have just travelled from London on the overnight train. I am bone weary. But by all means, let us talk."

She refused to lower herself to respond to his sarcasm. "I will make some tea," she said and strode ahead of him into the kitchen.

She heard him shut the front door. She heard him sigh, "Ah, yes, tea. The eternal nostrum."

In the kitchen, she gave herself willingly to the soothing rote of the tea-making. Fill the kettle. Light the gas. Fetch down the teapot and two mugs. Decant the loose tea into the tea egg, a fiddly process she normally avoided, preferring to plunk two tea bags in the pot. Now, she welcomed any activity that would fill up the time, slow the beat of her own blood. If the situation exploded, she must be ready to ride and steer her own passions. And indeed, her busy fussing with the preparations seemed to be working. Her blood and time itself were slowing down. Time slowed as one approached the speed of light, did it not? And perhaps in mere minutes, some revelation wrested from Murdo would pierce her brain with just that speed and clarity.

She heard the leather of his shoe soles slide over the flagstone floor, the slight scrape of the chair leg as he sat down. She turned round to find him looking full at her. He appeared completely composed, his hands folded on the table

in front of him. In the filtered light of the kitchen, his powerfully sculpted face was beautiful once again. She recalled
with some anguish the first time she had ever seen him,
across the room at a mandatory university sherry party. The
broad cheekbones, the full, sensual mouth. His age and quiet
dignity (or so it struck her then), which played upon his features like the last plangent note of an exquisite song of
mourning. This mane of burnished hair streaked with grey.
She had been drawn ineluctably to this man of tempered fire.
And whatever happened, she could not deny that the sex
between them had been magnificent.

*Sex is a powerhouse. Approach it with due caution and awe. For
misused, it can maim and kill.* Suzanne had understood her
mother to mean a pathology of both body and soul.

"Sit down, please, my dear. I shall tell you my side, shall
I?" This was Murdo's usual voice, calm and cultured.

"Let me say first, that I probably should have prepared
you for their poison. And it was somewhat cowardly of me
to leave. But as you no doubt learned all too well, my relations with my children could be no worse."

"I do recognize that I am in part to blame. Today I would
be charged, and perhaps rightly, with what psychologists
term a parenting deficit. I held my self distant from them, yes.
I was perhaps an excessive disciplinarian. I treated them as
my father treated me, and his father before him. If I am
guilty, it is there the guilt must lie. I did not make my affection manifest. Then of course, there were the untimely deaths
of Miranda and Kirstie. Both struck me terribly hard. I was
selfish, yes. I retreated from my own children. This was
doubtless unconscionably selfish. I left their care to others. To
hired nannies. To boarding schools. Of all this, I am guilty."

"I have in the past, earnestly tried for some reconcilia-
tion. I have apologized. I have tried to explain that I was
conditioned by the strictures of my upbringing. It has been
to no avail. With Clara, I have sometimes thought that I made

a little headway. But there too, I am ultimately defeated. By the very force of biology. Because Callum is her twin, she is bound to side with him against me. He is quite mad, as you doubtless grasped. He should long ago have been institutionalized, in my opinion. But we live in a mad time. He may well keep company with those who find his insanity normal. Drug takers, prostitutes, perverts of all kinds. God knows what sewers of humanity Callum trawls in."

Suzanne's hands had gone quite numb. Murdo's disquisition – for so it seemed to her – had the taint of rehearsal. Even for him, the phrasing was frigidly formal, "I did not make my affection manifest." Then too, his description of Callum was so widely off the mark, bore no resemblance whatsoever to the young man she had met. She felt again his tender mouth touching hers, his warm breath on her neck. She feared her face might show what she thought. The kettle began to whistle, and then to scream, and she got up, grateful for these minutes granted her to compose herself.

I feel no guilt about my attraction to Callum, she thought. Absolutely no guilt. What I do feel is a deep perplexity. Murdo is talking. This is what I wanted. Yet I do not think that I believe what he says. She poured the boiling water into the teapot. And then sat down again.

"Murdo," she began. "They told me…"

"Please, Suzanne, let me continue. I will tell *you* what they said. I know their concocted stories quite well by now, believe me. You see, they have done this before. They have attempted to poison my attachments to other women over the years. And often, to my sorrow, they have succeeded."

She had not expected this. Once again, she had failed to think of the women who had preceded her. For of course, there must have been others. After Kirstie died, and before her own encounter with Murdo, there might well have been countless others. Was it possible that she was simply the latest

in a long line of Murdo's "attachments" to whom the children deliberately fed disinformation? Yet how to reconcile
this possibility with Jeremy's evident probity, with Callum's
tears, with Clara's blithe transparency? Could they be so
practised at deception?

"I shall condense what I believe they told you. This
brevity is for my own sake. As I am sure you appreciate, I find
their lies unbearably painful."

"Let us get this over with, then. First, that I was somehow responsible for Miranda's death. That I kept her on a
starvation diet. That I took Jeremy away from her. The truth
is she was already ill when we married, although neither of
us knew it at the time. Had I known, I should have taken
precautions. I would never have let her become pregnant.
The birth itself nearly killed her. She could not have coped
with the demands of a baby. And Jeremy was an excessively
demanding baby. Just as he has grown into an excessively
demanding man."

"I ask you. How did the children arrive at their interpre-
tation of Miranda's decline? The twins did not yet exist.
Jeremy was less than a year old. Shall I tell you? This tale, like
all the others, is manufactured. Admittedly, Miranda's mother
played a role. The woman was a hysteric. It was she who first
put this nonsense into Jeremy's head. She always detested me.
Because had I not come along, Miranda would have been a
Bride of Christ. What a waste. Oh, my Miranda, what a
waste."

He put his head in his hands. Then emerged with an
apology. "Forgive me. That was unseemly."

Unseemly, Suzanne repeated to herself. What an odd
choice of words. As though he spoke to an outsider. Was this
a calculated defence then, primed to perfection? In Miranda's
journals, she thought, everything Jeremy said is substantiated.
But if I mention the journals, Murdo will blame illness or the
medication Miranda was taking. He will say her sickness had

made her unbalanced. What does it mean that I am sure he will say this?

She stood up then, a little shakily, to pour out the tea. She slid a mug over to Murdo, who grasped its base with both hands.

Suzanne put the mug to her lips, and sipped cautiously, wishing it were some faery brew that bestowed faultless discernment.

Murdo also drank. "Thank you, my dear." He wiped his brow with the back of his hand. "I will be so relieved to get this over with. I do not understand why they must go on tormenting me so. It is only my children who make me feel I am an old man."

He paused, as if waiting for her to deny this.

Suzanne kept silent, only willing the light to come at last.

"And so," he continued with a heaving sigh, "to the second of their fabrications. Kirstie's hang gliding. Their tale is that I encouraged her in this sport. That I was studying her flight – their shoddy reasoning quite defeats me here – to corroborate some theory about gravitation and the curvature of space. It is such nonsense, so terribly absurd, that it would be laughable were it not for the tragedy of Kirstie's death."

"The truth is that I hated her obsession with hang gliding. She would not be dissuaded. I went and watched her because I feared for her. It made me physically ill. My heart was in my mouth all the time she was in the air. But I had this foolish notion that if I always watched her, she would come to no harm."

He stopped and bowed his head.

And the picture, Suzanne wondered. What of the photograph you showed Callum? And then: what if there never were such a photograph?

Murdo took some very audible deep breaths; then sipped again at his tea. "Nearly done," he said. "Thank God. I cannot tell you how I detest this. I am sixty-two years old. You would think they might leave me in peace."

"Callum," he said and sat down his mug with a thud. "Callum. Child of my loins though I am hard pressed to admit it. Feckless, disruptive Callum. Who is at the root of all these machinations. For although he is insane, he is cunning. He is the viper in this family, the one who has convinced Clara and Jeremy that I am a monster."

Murdo's face was flushed. Suzanne was doubly on edge, concerned that Murdo might be on the verge of apoplexy, and herself stung by the image of Callum as viper. She had met vipers in her life, men and women both. She could see none of their maliciousness in the young Callum Napier. The eye, she thought. Murdo must mention Callum's eye.

"They told you, no doubt," he began, "that I am responsible for the idiot boy's blind eye. It is true that I held the hammer that wounded him. But the facts are these. He lunged at me like a mad bull, unthinking, unseeing, as is his wont. It was he who rammed his own bestial little face into the hammer. He had an ungodly strength for a child. Hyperactive, we were told. Hyper-everything, when it comes to Callum. He was the agent of his own blinding. Oh, unwittingly, of course. I do not suppose he was even aware I was holding a hammer."

"Callum has always had precious little grasp on reality. And all the drugs simply exacerbated his mania. LSD, MDA, Ecstasy. I lost count of the number of schools he was thrown out of because of drugs and other scrapes. It is a wonder to me that he can still cross a street and not get hit."

Suzanne waited for Murdo to qualify, even minimally, this horrendous wrapping up of his son. But nothing came. Murdo's self-defence was at an end. She understood this by the way he sat back in his chair. Erect. Satisfied. The lion has eaten a good meal. The lion knows his own truth. He has eaten it and finds it good. *Quod erat demonstrandum.*

Who is this Callum that Murdo speaks of? Is it a Callum Murdo has made up? Or is it a Callum that Callum himself has made up to torment his father? Is every family its own self-contained theatre? Or its own myth-making machine?

"Callum told me…" she began. Then winced as Murdo flung his mug to the floor. The china shattered. Tea seeped over the stone.

"Callum told you," he hissed. "So, the idiot speaks now? No babble for you, I gather. And what did Callum tell you?"

Never had she imagined that Murdo would appear ugly to her. Yet now he did. A ranting, florid, horrid old man.

"Calm yourself, Murdo, please. Let us simply leave it for now."

"Oh, I am calm, Suzanne. Deadly calm, in fact. Just tell me what that aberrant creature has invented now."

She felt she had no choice but to go on. "He told me you made him look at a photograph of Kirstie after she had fallen."

Murdo looked genuinely aghast. "My God, do you mean a photograph of her when she… No," he said. "I do not believe even he…"

He shook his head again and again, as if to fling the thought far away. "And do you really think I would do something so vilely sadistic? Or that I am so sick I would keep a picture of my beloved Kirstie, all… No, no. It is too much to bear. The boy is truly foul. Foul."

He put his head down on the table. His shoulders were trembling.

She regretted having spoken. She had not wanted to torture him in this way. Callum had lied to her about the photograph, then. Or perhaps he had a hallucination on drugs, which afterwards he took to be real. Murdo could not be feigning this distress. She had not meant to torture him.

She went to him and tentatively touched the back of his neck. He flung his arms about her hips and laid his head on

her belly. She was surprised to feel no wetness. She presumed
he had been crying.

She kept her hand on his shoulder until at last he
unlocked his grasp.

I cannot hug him back, she realized. I am still far too
wary. Something more has to happen. The clarity must come.

And so it did.

"I have come up with a plan," she heard Murdo say in his
habitually composed tones. "And perhaps now is the most
opportune time to speak of it. I have confessed to you my
fault. I admit I was a poor father. But you, dear Suzanne, can
give me the chance to make up for my past omissions."

Oh no, she thought. Not this. Surely not.

"I know, my dear," he went on with an indulgent smile,
"that you lied to me when you said you cannot have children. I know you better than you think. Procreation is a
realm we two must share. So, let us do this, Suzanne. You
can guide me, help me to be the father I should have
been."

I must speak rationally, she thought, although he is being
most irrational. "Murdo, I am not at all sure I want to be a
mother. To be frank, I had never even considered this when
we…"

"Well, my dear, consider it now. And for your sake. You
are thirty-four. There is the very real factor of the biological
clock. And motherhood is surely an experience every
woman must have."

"Why, Murdo? Why must every woman have this experience? If I choose not to have children, then it is indeed my
prerogative. You are being presumptuous."

"Let us not quarrel, Suzanne. There has been enough
stress for today, has there not? I think you will find your
instinct will override your intellect eventually."

He paused. She seethed, more at herself than at Murdo;
that she had not perceived this opacity in him.

"Is it a question of vanity, perhaps?" he persisted. "The stretch marks? Fear of drooping breasts?"

"What! Oh, do shut up, Murdo." Had he always read her so wrongly? His misapprehension would be laughable, were it not so sad.

Murdo is sad. The light had come at last. Murdo is a sad human being. He really does not see. Perhaps he really is as the children describe him. The ardent puppet master. The controller. He wants me pregnant, heavy with child. He does not really want a child. He wants me shaped to his will.

Murdo was speaking. Suzanne had to wrench herself back in order to listen. She was not at all sure she wanted to listen. Was this really Murdo speaking? Or some other voice from centuries ago?

"I understand women's vanity," Murdo was saying. "Miranda and Kirstie were just the same. But today's cosmetic surgery can completely eradicate any physical blight childbirth leaves on the body. Stretch marks all smoothed away. Breasts made firm. You could even have that nasty little mole on your back removed. You are probably yourself unaware of it. I don't mean to upset you, but I do find it off-putting. These little protuberances are vestigial nipples, you know. From our earlier mammalian days. Rather horribly bestial, when you think of it."

"I do not think of it, Murdo. I do not think of it at all. And I certainly will not go under the knife in order to satisfy your obsession with unmarked flesh."

I will tell him now. I will tell him I am leaving.

"Women are so terribly impulsive," Murdo said. In his face she read the manufactured indulgence one assumes with an unruly child.

"Do be reasonable, Suzanne. I certainly have no obsession with unmarked flesh, as you rather crudely put it. We have got off the point, haven't we? I mistook your hesitation, then. I apologize. The issue is obviously not vanity."

"I blame the children," he went on. "I do. We have not quarrelled before. They sow disaffection and mistrust. We must transcend their machinations. It would be best, I think, if we return to London tomorrow. They have infected this house for you, I believe."

The house is already infected, she thought.

"What do you say, Suzanne? Shall we set off tomorrow? I need a day to rest and then we shall leave. Leave their poison quite behind us."

"Murdo, I must go off on my own for a while. I need time to think."

She could smell his fear. He threw his arms about her waist, clung like a limpet. She willed herself not to struggle.

"Don't leave me, Suzanne. Don't leave me. I need you. With you, I can see the night skies again as I did when I was a young man. Through you, I can feel and see again. Don't leave me."

She felt she was choking. The room seemed to her to be full of smoke. I must get away. I must get away from this burning touch of his flesh.

She pushed him from her.

He sat back. The look on his face was stunned and disbelieving. Then anger seized him, so swiftly that Suzanne was not ready – not ready at all – when Murdo sprang to his feet, grabbed her upper arms, and wrenched her out of her chair. She winced, raised her hands to undo his grip on her. He grasped her tighter.

"What is it you damned women want?" His face was hideous in his rage. His teeth were bared. In their brightness, she thought of animals transfixed by car headlights. She was judging his exact distance from her, plotting her next move, when his hands moved suddenly to her shoulders, digging painfully into her collarbone. She knew with a terrible certainty that his fingers would shortly lock around her throat.

She kneed him sharply in the testicles. Murdo collapsed to the floor, winded, clutching his crotch.

She ran from the kitchen and shut the door behind her. She took the piece of paper from her pocket as she sped to the telephone in the front hallway. She prayed his pain would last long enough for her to make the call. Five digits. Her fingers shook as she punched the buttons.

It was a woman who answered. "Is Callum there, please?" She was amazed she managed to get the words out without stuttering. This is how Callum lost his ability to articulate, she thought. Murdo's brutishness foiled his tongue. She thought she heard Murdo groan.

"Suzanne?" The sound of Callum's voice was anodyne. Ada's pearl.

"I've been waiting for you to call. How bad is it? No, don't tell me. There's probably no time. Just get out of the house. Wait for me on the main road. And don't look back, Suzanne. I'll be less than twenty minutes."

As she put down the receiver, she heard Murdo push open the kitchen door. "Suzanne!" Yes, the cry was plaintive. He was gulping. He was still winded. She was not at all sorry.

She bounded up the stairs, two at a time, and grabbed her knapsack and sweater. On the way back down, she almost slipped in her haste. It is quite all right, she told herself. And of course, I can move faster. He must still catch his breath, find his car keys…

Halfway down the gravelled driveway, she did look back. He was standing in the front doorway, his arms flung outward, his hands clutching at the doorframe as if to keep his drooping body erect. His head was bowed. Then he looked up and saw her. He put an arm out to her, imploring.

She ran. She did not look back again.

She was still running when she heard the roar of the bike, that black beast and its rider who were the medium of her deliverance.

18

Defying Gravity

The sign at the start of the mountain pass is chillingly admonitory. "Do not attempt this road in rain or fog, particularly on motorbike. It is for experienced drivers only."

Callum has stopped the Triumph so that they can stretch their legs and look up at the mountains where the bike will shortly carry them over 2,000 feet. He has prepared her well. This is *Bealach na Bà*, the highest road in Scotland. Once a mountain pass for cattle. The narrow road zigzags. There are hairpin turns. The maximum gradient is one in four. At times, they will travel a slender ledge, above a drop of several hundred feet. She must inhabit her fear, wear it like armour. On this road, there will be no way to escape fear. The terror is a necessary part of the wonder.

When they reach the plateau, she will stand closer to the sky than ever before in her life. Beneath her, she will see the North Atlantic and the Isle of Skye as if they were new-made. As she wishes herself to be, by virtue of her contact with this place.

The English name for this whole fish-tail peninsula is Applecross. Which had reminded her uncomfortably of Eve's alleged sin and of the cross Murdo will not forego as a life prop. These are the shadow halves of myth, she thinks, that will pull us all down to hell if we embrace them.

But Callum has given her the old Gaelic name for the peninsula, which is *Comeraich*, a sanctuary. For centuries, this place was a recognized sanctuary for fugitives of all kinds.

She recognizes herself as a fugitive. She has run away from the man she married, in company with the son he calls imbecilic, less than human, an aberration. She thinks of Callum as a radiant boy. She is aware of the high price he has paid to keep his innocence. She knows that Murdo would not understand this.

A few hours ago, when they stopped at a cosy, white-washed café, she noticed for the first time the needle marks in his forearm. She touched the puncture marks gingerly and looked at him in silent question. "Never again," he said. She is amazed at what he has managed to accomplish. The slender ledges travelled. The ridgepoles walked. To make himself other than Murdo. Because there has always been the real danger that he might fall.

The danger presses now for both her and Callum as she mounts the bike behind him, then grips the passenger strap firmly in her right hand and the metal bar of the seat in her left. As they ascend the steep, twisting road through the mountains, she must sit erect, holding fast to the strap and the bar. She must make no sudden movement. She must not at all costs lean forward, so that her face is against his back, or her arms wrapped around his chest. If she lurches in panic, she could send them both to their deaths. She understands that Callum is trusting her with his life; that this risk is reciprocal.

He revs the bike and they rise so steeply, she fears they will slide backward. The fact is there is no way back. The narrow road allows no turning. They must go forward or perish. The road rises, and then twists, again and again, and again. The bike roars onward, a black beast on a slender ledge rising into the sky. What they are doing defies logic. It is as if gravity itself is a dark pounding heart against which they must pitch themselves.

She grips the strap. She grips the bar. And suddenly the armour of her fear is permeable. The wind in her face and the taste in her mouth is tart and sweet. She turns her head carefully and looks behind her. Far, far below, there is a lake, caught in the cleft of blue and amethyst mountains. She sees the rock and the harsh land hug the swift light to themselves. They are transformed even as she looks at them. The rock lives, as Ada said. If it would not mean her death and Callum's, she would like to stretch out her arm and touch the mountain on her left. It is that close. A sentinel of earth, obdurate yet mysteriously yielding. For the first time in her life, she actually sees how the mass of the world curves space. These mountains and the sky have a mystic and terrifying marriage. She and Callum are caught now in the fierceness of that bond; in the wild and terrible beauty of this place. They are riding a curvature of space, and the sky is so close she believes she inhabits its lilac-tinged clouds.

Rising and rising. Through mountains stern and solid, soft and young. Or is it she who feels young, so near to this throbbing power, this marriage of earth and sky? And then here is the ledge Callum warned her of. She looks down to the sheer drop below, to a well of glorious space and mesmerizing light. Where death waits, and life as well.

And now they are past it. She grips the strap and the bar. And they rise. At last the bike levels out and they stop at the gravelled edge of a rocky plateau.

Her ears are ringing, her legs numb as she gets off the bike. Callum has taken off his helmet. His eyes are bright. His hair is a turbulence of gold in the high wind. She takes off her own helmet. The wind seeks out her mouth and nostrils. She has to fight for breath.

Then she finds the right rhythm, a way to breathe while the wind batters her body. She walks out on to the plateau in

the direction of the light glittering up from the sea. This is the
bounty of desolation, for there is only rock and lichen and
sky. As she walks toward the edge to look down at the sea, the
wind drops a little. Cairns stand all around her, so precariously
made, she can hear the wind whisper between the spaces of
stone balanced on stone. The cairns are a human presence that
is also an absence. She looks back and sees Callum, still standing by his motorbike. Perhaps he is smoking a cigarette. She
understands he is deliberately letting her be.

She walks on and sees the blue body of Skye dreaming
in the Atlantic, and the light that comes up to her is a great
silver wheel.

Three thousand miles away, she thinks, my mother
walked into this same ocean because she was dying and
could not cure herself. And she hears her mother then,
through the whispering in the spaces of the cairns: "This is
your marriage. Only this."

As Suzanne stands there on the edge of the world, she
inhabits again the proud tower begun in her adolescence, the
keep compounded of the four elements. This earth she stands
on that is purest rock, this ocean that lies stretched beneath
her, and the unbounded sky above. And the fire out of which
all things are born. That is in her now, fierce and yet controlled.

Not a fire I allowed to be outside, lit at my feet and
climbing my thighs and making me writhe. That false fire
was only lust between me and Murdo. The false flame of his
hair and his heart and his meretricious show of suffering.
This is my marriage, she thinks, as she kneels down to lay a
cool grey oblong stone atop a cairn. I am restored to myself.

When she stands up, she sees Callum walking toward her,
his slim body utterly at peace with this place. He touches her
face, then passes her helmet for the journey down, where she
and he and the bike will hug the earth and all its nested
spells.

Epilogue

She has whitewashed the outside of the house to better catch and cast back the light from the sea. To protect her herbs from the whip of the wind and the flung salt air, she has mended the low stone wall bordering her garden

Suzanne has heard that there is a prehistoric forest somewhere in this cluster of islands. Otherwise, there are no trees. There is earth, and there is unyielding rock that moves nonetheless, working its image into her mind.

Last night, in a sheltered cove near the sea's edge, she lit a fire of garden brush. Then she paced out a square, recalling the proud watchtower of her adolescence. She has sought out this place where the Elementals congregate in full force. Her mother's words are a cloak against the eternal wind that haunts her new home: "Weather made the first gods."

Suzanne has begun to build a cairn. A stone for Gemma, who is now in Nigeria, working in a women's co-operative. One for Callum, who has had another exhibition and fallen in love with a young journalist he met through Jeremy. He has sent Suzanne a photograph of them together. Round their image she has cast a protective hoop, floating and invisible.

It was Callum who showed her how dramatic a leap was needed to escape Murdo's field of force. Suzanne wonders now if Murdo's obsession with the make-up of the stars was the root cause of his undoing. "Their density exceeds the average density of matter by a factor of ten to the twenty-seventh power." It was a fact that so fascinated him, he would repeat it like a mantra. Here was a number whose vastness Murdo's mind could perhaps entertain. But the idea of that unimaginable density hung about her body like lead.

"There are those whose very field of being can sicken or madden us." So her mother cautioned her when she was very young. Now Suzanne sees that the most pernicious of those human fields are innately duplicitous; they attract us through a projected image that is as irresistible as it is false.

"It is often not their fault, poor dears," said Ada. What mattered most was that Suzanne make her own intuitive body an instrument that could read where danger lurked.

One of her tasks here is to recall in full, and more vigilantly practise, her mother's counsel.

This morning Suzanne found the stone she recognized at once as Ada's. When wet, it is aquamarine. Dry, it turns a flecked grey-blue. An ellipse, smoothed by the endless churning of the sea, yet not completely so. The stone has a slight roughness which not even time and the sea have subsumed. As Ada had a grittiness, a singularity that could not be quelled.

Last night, Suzanne knelt by the cairn. In the hollows between the stones, the wind off the sea made a spirit song. Can there be such a thing as jubilant lamentation? That was the nature of the song.

She knows whose song this is. It is to them she will dedicate her book.